CLEANSED
by
DEATH

A Jo Oliver Thriller
Book One

CLEANSED
by
DEATH

A Jo Oliver Thriller
Book One

Catherine Finger

 Elk Lake
PUBLISHING, INC.

Plymouth, Massachusetts

Cover design: Derinda Babcock
Interior Design: Derinda Babcock
Editors: Erynn Newman, Deb Haggerty

PUBLISHED BY: Elk Lake Publishing, Inc., 35 Dogwood Dr., Plymouth, MA 02360

Library Cataloging Data
Names: Finger, Catherine (Catherine Finger)
Cleansed by Death—A Jo Oliver Thriller: Book One / Catherine Finger
204 pp. 23cm × 15cm (9in × 6 in.)
Description:
Identifiers: ISBN-13: 978-1-946638-66-3 (trade) | 978-1-946638-67-0 (POD) | 978-1-946638-68-7 (e-book.)
Key Words: Jo Oliver, police procedural, female protagonist, mystery/suspense, contemporary, serial killers
LCCN: 2018931772 Fiction

PRAISE FOR CATHERINE FINGER'S

CLEANSED BY DEATH

"This skillfully crafted suspense story of a police chief tracking a serial killer will have you on the edge of your seat. Readers will root for Josie as she struggles to do the right thing, not only in her relationships but as she searches for answers about God. Catherine Finger has crafted a feisty heroine in Chief Josie Oliver as well as a cast of fascinating support characters. Looking forward to Catherine's next book in the series."

—Patricia Bradley, award-winning author of
Shadows of the Past

"Move over Kinsey Malone, Josie is in the house! This police chief is not only a local leader but respected throughout her community of coworkers, friends and good neighbors. She manages to overcome personal challenges while still putting the bad guy behind bars and reconciling her relationship with 'the magnificent being.'"

—Elizabeth Martin Stearns, Waukegan Public Library

"As a pastor, I rarely see characters in books or on screen who wrestle with God in a way that feels like what I see every day. *Cleansed by Death* is the rare exception, a world where spirituality is real but not easy, where the tragedies and triumphs of life work together to form a cohesive whole. I recommend it to anyone who has wrestled with God ... and loves a good mystery!"

—**Gary Ricci**, Pastor of New Hope Christian Community Church in Round Lake Heights, IL

"This Glock-toting, heel-wearing, justice-driven heroine in *Cleansed by Death* had me from the start. Unrelenting action and witty dialog kept me loving this ride-along until the very last page. A must-read."

—**Joseph Sugarman**, Chairman of Blublocker Sunglass Corporation

DEDICATION PAGE

To the One Most High—my Magnificent Being

ACKNOWLEDGMENTS

In the words of C.S. Lewis, I feel "lucky beyond my desserts" for the love and faithfulness of my family and friends who buoyed me through this magnificent journey. Special thanks to Margo and Joe, and Jodie and Carl for generating key character studies and ideas. More special thanks to my beautiful niece Catherine—a better writer by far—and to her equally beautiful sisters for sharing their delight with me along the way. Really special thanks to my warrior nephew, Dan, who taught me how to fight and which weapons to use for which battles—especially when you want to win.

My dear friend Erynn Newman kept one hand on my shoulder while sharing her supernatural encouragement and editing gifts, and I am grateful. Her constancy improved my work.

Thank you to my readers! Your enthusiasm spurs my passion for storytelling and strengthens my writing.

CHAPTER ONE

Thursday, December 10

Despite the fact that Christmas was fast approaching, traffic was smooth sailing on I-94 northbound. But what thoughts crept sluggishly through the murky caverns of my husband's mind? His large hands kept a death-grip on the wheel, like an Airborne corpsman gripping a jump-seat handle a second before free fall begins. We surged ahead over snowy Wisconsin roads, his fingers taut.

"Del, please slow down. It's snowing pretty hard out there." My stomach clenched and my temples tightened.

He rolled his eyes and shook his head. "Oh, so now you're telling me how to drive too? I don't think so."

He punched the accelerator, rocketing the car to well over eighty on the slippery highway. Would we make the exit up ahead intact? Clenching my teeth, I sank into silent compliance once again. I closed my eyes. The misery between us pressed in on me. We'd just made the turnoff when my cell phone buzzed.

"Oliver." I fidgeted with the seat warmer as I answered, my voice flat.

"Josie?"

"Yeah. Hey, Nick." The day we met, I'd been assigned to be his on-the-job training-wheels, his Field Training Officer, when all I had on him were a few months and my killer political instincts. Lucky me. We were scrungy beat cops together in Chicago. We were young, foolish, and thought we knew it all. Not much had changed, other than me staying close to home and him taking one undercover assignment after another until he morphed into a Fed. I smiled looking back, but in the next moment, I stiffened as my body slammed into the door panel. Del was taking this corner dangerously fast. I shut my eyes again and concentrated on Nick's voice as the car jetted forward. "What's up?"

"We got another vic. And they're getting closer to home. This is not cool." His silky voice hardened as he spoke.

"What do you mean? I thought you said the last murder happened in Spokane. That's not exactly next door. Was this one as bad?"

"Worse. And I'm talking about the current tragedy, not the last one. This one happened last night, early this morning technically, in Madison. Popped up on ViCAP right away. You on the road right now?"

"Uh-huh."

"You with the man?"

"Does it matter?"

"It matters to me, Josie. You matter to me. He's not driving, is he?"

"Yup."

"He knows you're talking to me."

It wasn't really a question. "Yup."

Nick Vitallero, at it again. My marriage should be off-limits. I loved the man beside me—wounds and all. Even if no one else did. Even if doing so made me almost as sick as he was. Am I sick enough to stay? I hope not. "Give me some info. How did the killer get from Spokane to Wisconsin?"

"Who knows? We haven't exactly cracked his travel schedule, but everything else is right in line. He grabbed a woman—a church mentor. She'd been working with a six-year-old girl through a formal mentorship program for the past

2

year. Successful woman. High profile attorney. Well liked, by all accounts. Everything to live for. And everything about the kill says it's our guy."

"Please tell me they found traces of drugs. Any kind of tranq in her system?"

"Not a one. She was most likely awake through the worst. He's escalating, getting more twisted. We're on high alert, and we want you in our inner circle. We need your hunting skills. In fact, the Governor of Wisconsin has also requested your participation. Let me sketch it out for you."

I'd given up on the Feds forever ago—but that didn't stop them from asking for my help occasionally. Every now and then I'd get an offer I couldn't refuse.

Del glared at me and then looked back at the road, his hands clenched. Anger glimmered in his eyes. Why had I given up that once-in-a-lifetime career offer with the Feds, tracking notorious criminals? Now Nick had all the glory—and all I had was Del. Nick revealed the brutality of another innocent woman's death at the hands of this twisted serial killer. I sucked in fresh air as he described the horror of the woman's last minutes alive.

I waited until he finished with the grim details, and then I exhaled hard and fast. Surely Del could sense my discomfort. Was he going to start hammering me again over why I'd stayed in the bush leagues by marrying a beat cop instead of marrying Nick all those years ago? I couldn't tell what he was thinking any more. When had I stopped trying?

Del smiled darkly but waited to act out until I ended the call and dropped the phone into the console compartment. "That your big-shot boyfriend again?"

Del's menacing tone sent a wave of nausea through me.

"He's not my boyfriend. There's been another murder. It ain't pretty." I closed my eyes, gently shaking my head.

CHAPTER TWO

Thursday, December 10

We crested a little hill and hit a patch of ice. Del's jaw went rigid as he battled the wheel. I gripped his thigh, but he grunted and shrugged me off.

I had chosen him—the out-of-control man in my car—over the possibilities of a life with Nick. Why?

The car slid and the traction control system made its own adjustments, trying to keep the car safely moving forward. All the average driver had to do, in theory, was reduce speed and allow the automated steering system to take over. Del had never been average. When the car moved of its own accord, he floored the gas instead of the brake. The jerky acceleration and his wrestling match with the steering wheel sent us off the road, sliding down a steep incline that must have been at least a hundred feet long.

Nick's handsome face appeared, abruptly pulled down like a shade and then ripped away by a fiery-faced Del, screaming beside me as we slithered down the hill. My heart pounded and heat swept through me, melting my lips together, shoving words back down my throat before they reached my tongue. I kept my mouth shut. All he had to do was let up on the gas, ease up on the steering wheel, and let the computers adjust the skid. Instead, he kept accelerating and forcing the wheel in the opposite direction. If we died, I would miss my friends, my job, my horse. But most of all, I would miss Samantha, the foster child I desperately wanted to adopt.

"Del, ease up on the gas. Don't fight the wheel for just a second. Relax." I spoke to him in quiet tones to soothe him out of his black mood as he spun the wheel back and forth. We continued to slide down the embankment.

"Shut up, Jo! We're locked in a skid! I'm not your pretty-boy FBI agent. I know how to drive! There's nothing else I can do!"

I shrank against the car door, shoulders hunched, head down. There's plenty he could do. *Take control, Oliver! You're a police chief! No, I should just walk away. Why couldn't Del hold me, care for me?* I stared at my knees, as if in a trace. If I was small and quiet enough, maybe he would calm down.

God, are You out there? Do You even exist? Why aren't You helping me? Some prayer that was, selfish and hollow. I did not want to die like this. But did I want to be saved, just to go through this again? So I sat there, holding onto the passenger door armrest with my right hand, bracing the other on the dash, shaking. I took a deep breath and steeled myself for what might come next.

I let out a sigh when we finally reached the bottom of the hill with a jolt—sideways, but intact. We ended up in a gully between a farm road and a large field, heading into a little stand of ancient pine and oak trees. I looked over at Del. His stony, impassive stare was followed quick as lightning by a hideous mask of anger. I was in deep, deep trouble.

He punched the accelerator again, letting up on the wheel long enough for the thing to self-correct, until we were parallel to the highway far above, moving along the dirt path, hitting pothole after pothole. He sped up when the trail faded into open fields and rural countryside. An old farmhouse rose above a ridge a few minutes beyond the end of the path. We might've been okay if he would have just kept driving straight.

I stared into the distance. A glimpse of Nick, smiling. Then the sweet smell of Samantha's hair as she rested next to me during a longer-than-usual Sunday sermon. I hadn't been to church since I was a small child until Samantha asked me to take her as often as I could. She had more faith than I. Which wasn't hard since I was pretty much an agnostic. An iron fist twirled through my stomach. *Shoulda, woulda, coulda.* Why hadn't I pushed past Del's resistance and adopted Samantha out of the foster care system? I wanted a child. A child of my heart.

Del accelerated even more, pushing to over seventy miles per hour on the rocky, frozen earth. Just as we came across pavement to end our off-road adventure, he snarled at me and turned the wheel sharply to the right, heading the nose of the car toward a thick patch of mature trees on my side. This couldn't be happening. He wouldn't. He couldn't, could he?

He steered the car straight toward the trees, zeroing in on a large, sturdy trunk, standing maybe thirty feet high, thicker than a tractor tire. I tried to relax into it, bracing for impact. The violent jolt of the fender glancing off the massive tree barely slowed us down, tearing into my passenger door. Airbags exploded and metal sheets folded like foil, but the steel frame protected me like a mama bird folded around her brood.

"My nose! I think it's broken!"

I recoiled from Del's shrill screams. His side of the car hadn't been touched, though his airbag had deployed. He was shaking theatrically—near tears. He got out of the vehicle, limping. He never once looked back at me, never tried to help me get out of the wreckage, never asked if I was okay.

The car door on my side was shredded. The handle wouldn't budge. I threw my shoulder into the door and a shard of glass cut into my skin. Blood seeped through the outer layers of my clothing and dripped onto the car seat. Fine white powder from the airbags settled, clotting blood on the door's upholstery.

I unbuckled my seat belt and pushed my seat backward to free my legs from under the wrecked dash. My stomach lurched at the acrid stench dominating the car's interior. Del barked orders into his cell phone as I hoisted myself over the console toward the open driver's door. Once he ended the call, our eyes locked, and for a split second he gave a triumphant smile.

I had to get out of my marriage—the sooner the better—if I wanted to get out alive.

CHAPTER THREE

Thursday, December 10

I grabbed the steering wheel for leverage and the car lurched to the right, throwing me down onto Del's heated seat. I sat back, panting. Thin streams of blood dripped onto the warm leather from my jacket sleeve. Pain knifed through me with each heartbeat. Fuzzy stars ebbed and flowed in front of my eyes. I pressed my right hand into the crimsoned leather seat and grabbed the steering wheel with my left hand to steady myself. A thin film of talcum powder from the depleted airbags covered the palm of my hand.

I blinked my eyes several times to stop the dash from rushing toward me and receding back like a sea at low tide. The radio crackled on with the low-slung voice of some female crooner.

I turned off the radio, then opened the console and jammed my hand inside, searching for my cell phone. My fingers bumped into a checkbook, a brush, and a pack of gum before grasping the plastic cover. I pulled the phone out and slid it into my coat pocket. I took in another deep breath, closed my eyes, and edged myself with glacial slowness over the warm seat to the door. My left foot hit the ground, and I turned my hips to wrench my right leg out of the car. I pushed myself up. Vertigo rocked me from side-to-side as I staggered onto the road.

Del's face was bathed in blue light when the first squad car responded to the accident.

With shaking hands, I tapped the first picture in my faves' contact list and waited for Nick to answer. Icy wind battered my matted hair. Del's anger steamed from both eyes. We locked eyes, and a rogue tear trickled down my face. I stabbed at my face with my bloody right hand. Nick picked up, and I turned away from my husband.

"Another Josie call. Miss me?"

The muscles at the base of my neck relaxed. I closed my eyes and breathed lightly into the phone.

"Josie? Whatever it is—I got you."

"Come. Nick, I need you to come get me. Now."

"You still in Wisconsin?"

"Yeah. At the end of the road with Del. He just plowed the car into a tree. On my side of the car. By accident ... maybe ... maybe not. Just come. Please."

"Cops there?"

"Yeah."

"Don't worry. I'll find you. Then I'll find Del."

Nick waited for me at the emergency room registration desk, his jaw tight. "So, it's true?"

I nodded.

"Cops say you didn't file a report. Didn't give a statement."

I shrugged. Welcoming waves of hospital-strength painkillers lapped up my anxiety. Things struck me as almost funny. The neat stitches sewn into my shoulder resembled a nice butter braid, an image that made me hungry. But I smiled and suffered in silence.

"Let's get out of here so you can rest, and we'll talk about this later." Nick's voice was sweet like warm apple cider.

I was dying for some quality chocolate. But I didn't mention it. Instead, I leaned into Nick, struggling to stay awake as I stumbled through the parking lot. He opened his car door and gently lifted me in. His earthy scent wafted above me as he leaned over to buckle me up. I inhaled deeply and smiled before drifting off to sleep.

Safe.

ish me luck, amigo." I kissed Gino on the cheek and slid out of the car.

"My prayers and my heart are always with you, *mija*. Though this time, I'll be there too. In the shadows." He winked as I closed the door and nodded at him.

"What are you waiting for?" I buckled my seatbelt and stared at Hector impatiently. "He's waiting for us to pull out." Adrenaline coursed through me. "This ain't *my* first rodeo, Jaime. So, jump out in front and don't spare the horses."

Hector shook his head and drove the last few miles while hopefully soaking in all the useful cover details I spouted about horses, hicks, and life at the track. Hillsboro sprang up before us. A row of buildings that had seen better days ushered us to a stop sign.

"Main Street. Man, I love small town America. Which way, Chief?" The edge in Hector's voice generated waves of energy.

I took a deep breath, driving my thoughts back to high school and summer days full of horses and flirting with cute cowboys. "Turn left, go on down the road a good six or seven blocks and pull up into an angled parking spot on the right hand side of the road. The auction house will be on the other side of the street." Sudden assurance floated over me, and I knew beyond a shadow of a doubt that we were in the right place, at the right time. Burdock was here. I could feel it.

CHAPTER FOUR

Friday, December 11

The killer, wiry and strong, appeared and disappeared like lights flickering in a storm. He had started out as a harmless presence in my dream. Sometimes a solid form, sometimes a whisper of a man—always floating above and circling what looked like playgrounds.

He orbited far away from the women and children chattering happily below him. But then his flight would grow urgent, morphing into a tangible cloud of malevolence. His mouth spewed filth as he descended, distorting his features. He pulled himself closer to the unsuspecting children and women with each spiral. Close enough to touch them.

Heart pounding, I tried to warn them, but I couldn't speak. I couldn't move.

When I finally managed to croak out a semblance of a warning, the little girls turned with one face, and I scratched my throat raw with a silent scream. I knew her. All the women turned to look at me, their eyes chilling me to the bone. They were all a different version of me. The killer still circled, coming nearer and nearer, evil coating and coursing out of him like boiling lava. Mercifully, I woke up. Alive. And alone.

Disturbing images hung like wisps of spider silk. I eased to a sitting position. I needed to remember, to make sense of the frightening, now receding, scenes. I shook my head—a bad move. The pounding in my temples rivaled the pain that wracked my body, especially on my right side. An encounter with a dump truck would've been welcome right about now. Anything to kill the pain.

I stared into space for a good five minutes. The mule deer rack hanging on the wall in front of me wouldn't have been my first choice of wall art. This was not my own bed at home. I was still in Wisconsin. Alone. More or less. Nick's leather jacket hung on the doorknob to the adjoining motel room. The door was slightly ajar, and an Italian aria whispered into my room from his. Mystery solved.

Del had rented a separate room last night after the "accident." So had Nick—right next to mine. Bad cop, good cop, on steroids. Tiny swords sliced into my temple at the thought of Del somewhere nearby. But Nick was right next door. His nearness was as deeply soothing as a warm, lavender oil-scented bath on a cold night. I swung my legs over the edge of the rickety "resort" bed. If only I had a normal marriage. Or at least a safe one. But I would be better off without Del, especially this morning.

Images of sliding down the hill and slamming into the tree tangled and merged. Accident? Intentional? Details swam in an inky pool of conjecture when I tried to dissect the traumatic event. No. I couldn't go down that path. I pushed the repugnant thoughts aside to focus on Nick's serial killer.

What motivated the Mentor Sister Serial Killer? In order to stop him, we needed to find the key to his choice of victims. Nick's description of the crime-scene photos merged with snippets from last night, oppressing my spirit with a weight that would've taken Atlas down.

Something Nick had said about this latest murder niggled at me. A connection hovered out of reach, teasing my subconscious. Something about why the Governor of Wisconsin wanted me involved in this case. Why me, a small-town police chief? Was this just a function of our small town roots pulling me back to the capital? Or did the governor really need my help?

I'd let it settle in and bubble up when the time was right.

Two years ago, slogging through mounds of data during a spree of gruesome murders, endless nights of pouring over reports, witness statements, crime-scene photos, and psych evals had strained me to the point of breaking. Another one of Nick's "consult jobs." My world had tilted more off kilter with each savaged child. I had sat beside each and every grieving parent, soaking up clues, tones, and possibilities. Desperately racing an unknown killer, I had nearly joined my colleagues in defeat.

Until my dreams wove into my daytime musings. Jarring bits and pieces from my dreams had pressed against me until a pattern emerged among the pictures in my head. Some bit of wisdom buried deep inside had led me to the key that unlocked the rituals the killer played out with his victims. That intuition led us to his door ... before a sixth child was taken.

There'd been many times over the course of my life when I felt and saw things in my mind's eye before they actually occurred. I'd come to trust this, even if I couldn't explain. All I had to do was go about my business, relax into the rhythm of a new day, and the insight would find me. And that led me straight back to Nick.

I'd reached out to him last night, and he had appeared. He had my back. I imagined his handsome, square face above a steaming mug of his perfectly-brewed French roast coffee. The familiar longing tried to settle in. I had to knock it off before I started seeing apparitions of the guy wearing my apron and bringing me breakfast in bed. And maybe toting my Glock, fully loaded.

A shower might help. Hot water washing over me for a good, long time would help me face what lay ahead. I grabbed my cell and listened to my voice mail. Speak of the handsome devil.

Nick had already left three messages, telling me in the last one he was going to pick me up, citing the name and address of our destination for the day. I looked at the fragile door between our two rooms. My eyes traveled over to the deadbolt. Best to get that baby locked. I called him back, and he told me Governor Burke wanted to see us as soon as possible. Since I had no car, Nick said he'd drive.

What had I said or done to him while under the influence of some pretty hefty painkillers? Vague images of him bending over me with warm, loving eyes plagued me. Had I kissed him? Hopefully not. Did it count if I couldn't remember it? I sort of hoped I had kissed him. Sort of. Mostly not.

My cheeks warmed and I bent my head, gritting my teeth. I had to get these thoughts and feelings under control. I am not going there. I'm a married woman. For now. Focus on work. Focus on the serial killer case.

The FBI only called Nick in when they were up against a multi-state monster that only the best could catch. He had top-flight law enforcement experience. How he'd landed in Washington, DC, as some sort of secret agent after the Special Forces and the Chicago PD had their way with him was still a mystery he kept from me. That was how Nick rolled.

Given the gaps in my understanding of his career trajectory, him being assigned to meet with Governor Burke this morning seemed like one more "tell" to me, but who knew? I had my own connection to the state capital, but it wasn't that big a secret. Wisconsin is really just a series of small towns strung together, like beads on a necklace. When it came right down to it, I was practically related to, or had gone to school with someone related to, every other person in the state.

The killer's dirty work in Wisconsin had both sides of the aisle in the state's capital in an uproar. Governor Burke himself wanted to meet with the core team, and by executive order, that now included me. Nick had wanted to give me a pass when he saw my condition last night, but I wouldn't hear of it.

Knowing I'd been summoned to the governor's office with Nick had undoubtedly fueled Del's early morning silence. Which was preferable to last night's ugly scene at the hospital when Nick had showed up in the emergency room. Del's angry bellow had been the only warning before he rushed Nick, completely forgetting his supposed injuries. Orderlies had jumped in and grabbed Del's arms while Nick stood by my side, steely eyes burning into my husband with disdain. When the orderlies muscled Del away, Nick just shook his head and made a tsking sound.

Last night, painkillers had seemed to do my marriage a world of good. Might've just been me though, come to think of it. I tried to shrug with my one good shoulder, dismissing the conflicting thoughts about my two main men as I made my way to the bathroom.

That wasn't my best move of the morning. I'd forgotten how much my punctured shoulder ached, but I remembered as soon as I shed the T-shirt I'd worn to bed and shuffled over the thick, shag carpet. The throbbing nerve signals in my muscles felt like hot pokers, and I gasped. But I needed to wash my hair and get presentable before meeting with the brass.

And I cared what Nick thought of my appearance. I managed to wash my hair and protect the bandages. Somewhat. It took a lot more effort than I'd have liked but was definitely worth it.

Once I finished my morning routine, grateful to whomever had brought my bags from our wrecked SUV to my room, I searched for Del to confront him before I spent the day hunting killers and holding politicians' hands with Nick. I found my husband in the diner next door, eating breakfast and holding court with a small group of locals. As I made my entrance, he was giving fantastic, faux details of the crash, making him out to be the hero in some wild, man-against-nature adventure.

So this was how it was going to be. Again.

I puffed out a breath of air and rolled my eyes. Swallowing bile, I turned away from the whole lot and sat down by myself at the other end of the counter. They knew who I was. They took Del's lead and ignored me. Another set of silent witnesses to my not-so-secret misery. Then Nick walked into the diner, singing in Italian and smiling with his perfect, white teeth.

Nick Vitallero was as gorgeous this morning at thirty-six as he had been at twenty-six. No, scratch that. He was actually better looking. A touch of gray at the temples set off his jet-black hair. A perfectly formed, square jaw framed his museum-quality Italian features. And he was as dangerously fit as ever.

Oh, boy. I'm gonna need another painkiller. STAT.

I ordered sausage, eggs, and toast, and turned away from Del and his new buddies as Nick slid onto the stool next to me. He winked at the waitress.

She smiled at him expectantly. "What'll it be, hon?"

"I'll have what she's having, with a side of you for supper. Say, about nine o'clock tonight?"

She rolled her eyes, snapped her order book shut and moved off, still smiling.

"Gotta hand it to you, Nick. You still got it."

"Yes, I do, Jo. I've got everything but you. Which was painfully obvious last night. You didn't have to alert every local yokel within a hundred miles. You called me. That was enough. I would've been happy to take care of you. And Del."

"I couldn't not call in the car accident ... you know that. I forgot what it was like in a hick town. I should've thought about the fact that something like this would be the biggest event this side of the state fair for those guys. Why do you think I blew this pop stand the minute I got out of high school?" The levity I forced into my voice wasn't working. Nick's face was an angry wall.

"So you bring the keystone cops to the scene from four counties but don't tell any of them about that scumbag of a husband of yours?"

"Sarcasm is beneath you, Nick." I patted his hand.

"Maybe so. But anger isn't. You grew up with half of those guys. As many times as you and your friends out-ran cops during your own crazy years, you couldn't pull one of them aside and tell them the truth? I guess I should be glad I'm not the only one you won't let behind those thick walls of yours." He reached his hand over and wrapped his fingers around mine.

"I'm doing the best I can, Nick. And no—I wasn't about to come clean to my old pals. Stealing for-sale signs and getting hauled in to the station together twenty years ago doesn't exactly make them my soulmates. There's no way I'd ever broadcast my wreck of a marriage to those dudes. Heck, three of them went from being tossed into the back of the squad to driving one within months of me taking the oath." I chuckled.

"It certainly didn't hurt that your sheriff responded to Del's call. The minute he showed up, I hear Del went gentle as a kitten. I still want to punch Del in the face." Nick's casual tone was a clue. He always grew unnaturally quiet when he was jealous.

"You know Quinn and I go way back." I eased my hand out from under his as our food arrived. "Can't say I didn't love the way he made a beeline over to me, completely ignoring Del."

"Quinn's too good a cop to buy your 'accident' explanation, but even in your weakened state, you charmed him into skimping the report. He told me you were like two little kids laughing about old times in the back of that ambulance, lights on and sirens off. It was ridiculous." He snorted in laughter. I'd won him back.

"I plead temporary insanity. I found my Sheriff Quinn to be both amusing and a perfect gentleman." I stabbed at my sausage and looked up at Nick.

"Someone should've chaperoned you two. I should've been there to defend your honor. Kept it from turning into a redneck reunion." He laughed again and shook his head.

"Laugh if you must, but his phone call did get us to the hospital in record time."

CHAPTER FIVE

Friday, December 11

I'd barely made it back to my room to grab my belongings before Nick's distinctive knock sounded at my door. I stood on the other side, trembling. As much as my heart sang at the thought of examining the evidence with him and going after a killer together, the mere idea of being alone in his car with him all day was throwing my body into meltdown.

Without all the distractions, would his laser mind cut through my denial of Del's motivation in the 'accident'? Even as we hunted a killer, Nick would chase down the truth about my crumbling marriage. Was that really what I wanted? To share with Nick the latest chapter of my gruesome love-story-gone-wrong?

I was sick of bearing secret agonies. Sick of living in isolation with nothing but the weight of my shame to rely on. Sick of slogging through the dregs of my unhappiness on my way out the door every morning, tiptoeing home every evening and hoping I'd make it through another day. Mostly though, I was sick to death of what was true about me and my abusive husband, and I was ready to find a new life. But could Nick guide me to the truth I sought? I stood there, unable to open the door.

Finally, I peeked through the door's peephole.

"Hey, beautiful! Do I have to invite myself in?"

Opening the door, I stood aside. He pulled me into his arms as soon as he crossed the threshold, mindful of my bandages. I leaned into him. He tightened his grip around my waist and back, pulling me closer. The feel of him, the smell of him, the solid truth of him poured over me, Maui-perfect. Darkness weaved in and out between the two of us, standing side by side in my mind's eye for a moment. I was a painfully married woman. Nick was my best friend. And long ago, he'd once been far more. But I couldn't think about that now. I pushed gently away from his embrace, reaching for some balance between us.

"I'm so glad you found me last night." I sighed.

"I've never lost track of you, beautiful, and I never will. Don't you know that yet? After all these years? Honey, you're always in my scope."

"Nick." His name poured off my lips like a smile. The warmth and safety of his arms set fire to a potent mixture of raw emotions. My heart went into overdrive, and my windpipe constricted. Every cell in my body thrummed with a distant sense of pleasure. So refreshing after my failure of a marriage. I wanted to be loved ... not abused.

I dropped my gaze to the porch decking outside my motel door as a wave of guilt washed over me. Should I even try to conjure up the courage to talk about what was happening in my shipwreck of a marriage or was that way out of bounds? As much as I respected Nick's opinion, mostly I just wanted an escape.

Was someone above looking out for me? Maybe my life could be bigger than this lousy moment in time, bigger than another wounded night by my abusive husband's side. Could I possibly have a guardian angel, and did I even believe in them? Bigger gun, better question—did I even believe in God?

One thing was for sure though—if I had a guardian angel, he was Italian, and his name was Nick.

CHAPTER SIX

Friday, December 11

Olive skin wrapped the muscle of Nick's right arm like water over solid rock in a Colorado river as he navigated the curved road one-handed. Judging by the slow upturn of his perfectly sculpted lips, he must've felt me watching him. I tried to pull my eyes away and content myself with staring out the window, but there was nothing to see but black-and-gray blobs speeding by as we glided down I-94 South toward Madison. Back to Nick.

He cracked a crooked smile. "You shoulda married me, Josie. You could watch me all day long."

My smirk and an eye roll were all I had to offer. We'd been down that road—half-joking and half-serious—many times before. We'd come closest to the altar years ago when we made it through our first few nerve-racking years as inner-city beat cops. He was my whole world once. Until he walked out on me with no explanation, leaving me keening for him like a she-wolf, night after night for longer than I wanted to admit.

Then Del waltzed into my life. Del with his Midwestern roots, non-stop charm, and black, souped-up sports car. But I didn't need to invite in the fantasy of Nick this morning. I needed more than the fantasy. I needed Nick next to me in the line of fire. So I needed to remain all-business. Maybe I could give myself extra credit for keeping my feelings for him on a low simmer?

I swallowed. "Yeah, yeah. Shut up and drive."

"That's what I love about you. No guesswork."

"Nope."

"Every man's dream."

"Yup. Well, turns out not every man's dream."

"So, are you ready to talk about it?"

"Guess not." I really thought I was, but once we were alone and driving along a quiet highway, I couldn't give voice to this. I couldn't speak the words that needed to be said. Instead, I kept staring at his wrist bone as he drove. Smooth.

Nick moved his hand toward me slowly and rested it on my shoulder. "Josie, there isn't anything you could tell me I haven't already guessed."

He widened his fingers and massaged my neck.

Warmth from his hand poured over me, crashing through my gut where it was met with a roiling sea. Heat rolled up my throat to my face. Twinkling pinpricks appeared before my eyes, and my lungs slammed into my ribs, leaving me gasping. I sat in silence. Surely my body would return to my control eventually. The car had stopped moving. Nick had pulled into a rest area, and I hadn't even noticed.

He unbuckled his seatbelt and turned to face me. "Josie, what happened between you and Del? What's really going on?"

His voice was low and steady.

A tear rolled down my cheek, and I turned to look out the window. I put my hand over his, kept my eyes focused on a fence post and began to speak.

"Shortly after we were married ten years ago, a couple of weeks maybe, we were driving on this very highway, fighting. The funny thing is, I don't even remember what about. We weren't even really fighting about anything, but we were fighting. And he was driving way too fast, like he does. And all of a sudden, going way over the speed limit, he pulls the car into one of those wayside stops. Without warning.

"I can still taste the bitter fear that came over me that day. He slammed on the brakes and sent the car skidding to a stop. He was shouting. I don't even remember what he was saying, but he was shouting."

I paused. Two small girls walked a dog through the dirt toward the designated pet area. They didn't seem old enough to read. How old did you have to be to read these days anyway? Nick kept his hand steady on my shoulder, his rhythmic breathing hypnotic. Oh, how I longed to turn around and lean into his arms. My heartbeat raced and I kept my eyes trained on the fence post, taking deep breaths and counting backward.

"The next thing I knew, he was grabbing me by the shoulders, hard, shaking me, yelling at me, saying crazy things. I was so shocked; I didn't even respond. I think that made him madder. He shrank away from me, but he kept yelling. And then he pulled his heavy set of keys out of the ignition and threw them. Right at my head. They hit the edge of the passenger window hard enough to crack it. And that's what stopped him.

"He got out of the car, still yelling, wanting me to drive. I climbed over and closed his door, and then I locked him out. I didn't even think about it, I just locked all the doors."

I drew in and held a deep breath as long as I could. My face was hot enough to fry an egg and the pulsing of my heartbeat in my temples was an out-of-control bass drum set.

"He got so mad he started kicking the doors in. Put a dent in the passenger door of his brand-new coupe. Something snapped inside of me, and I did something really wrong that day, Nick. Something I've been ashamed of ever since."

I finally turned glistening eyes to face him.

He cupped my face in his hand, and I read the heartbreak in his eyes. "What did you do, Josie?"

I locked my eyes on his, the unleashed shame leaking away. "I let him back in."

———————⟳⟲———————

Twenty minutes later, we were back on the road, bottles of water in hand and the talk of all talks momentarily behind us. I'd finally broken the dam, but that was all I could handle for today. Probably for tomorrow, too. I steered us back to something I could talk about and breathe at the same time—the murders.

"So, why me?"

"What do you mean?"

"Why include me in this investigation? I mean, I appreciate the professional courtesy, but why are you bending the ear of a small-town police chief to help you solve a murder one state over? What's up with that?"

"You've got a good nose for this kind of stuff. You're one of the few people I know with the both the guts and the brains to track a killer like this and to help me find the connections between the kills. We've been talking about the case since the murders started, and your gut hasn't failed me so far. You were the first one to wonder out loud if these cases were connected. You were the one to notice the little girl factor. And since the FBI's second-best solve rate is off on another case, I'm sticking with you. Despite the fact, that for a brilliant woman, you sure can be slow on the uptake sometimes."

"Could be we've seen one too many bad movies. Could be we're making up connections where there aren't any." I wasn't about to ask him to cut me any slack or remind him I wasn't exactly a hundred percent today.

"I don't think so. This case, the Mad Town Massacre, as the press is already calling it, is singing. Loud and clear. It's the same guy. And there's plenty about the situation you're not going to like, my friend."

"Such as?"

"You're catching the killer's geography, right?"

"Huh? Geography?"

His deep sigh seemed legit, and a wiser woman would've stopped there and thought it through. I barreled on. "What do you mean by 'geography'?"

"Last murder. Spokane, right? And the gruesome one before in LA, remember?"

"Sure ... the Spokane murder was in Lilac City, not too far from where my sis lives. And yes, I've got a niece in LA. I haven't forgotten. So?"

His uncharacteristic eye roll seemed like a clue, but about what? I might've picked up on it had I not been suffering from last night's trauma.

"So ... Madison, new crime scene, same perp."

"Yeah, I know. We're headed there now. So?" I shifted in my bucket seat.

"Didn't you go to school in Madison for a day or two? And you've just admitted your small-town ties to the gov." He gestured to me with his right hand, completing his sentence in true Italian fashion.

"See, now that's exactly what I'm talking about. Don't you think that's a bit of a stretch? My nearly one whole year at UW Madison and family members in LA and Spokane does not a crime nexus make. And I've gone to high school or college with lots of people. That means nothing. You need to admit it. You missed me and drew me into this to get the opportunity to sharpen your skills. Just like the good ole days." I playfully punched his shoulder.

He snorted and smiled, ignoring my comment as he soldiered on. "So, is it safe to assume you have neither a plan nor any ideas to offer up along with our condolences when we meet with the grieving governor in a little less than an hour?"

"Condolences? As in, on behalf of the police force? What condolences?"

Nick's energy shifted. He stared straight ahead for a good two or three miles, and when he finally spoke, he kept his words measured and slow. "There are a few anomalies in this case I thought you might have already discovered."

"Yeah? Go on."

"This one hits pretty close to home." He sighed and eased up on the gas.

"As in Madison? Because I went to high school with Governor Burke? That kind of close to home? Is that what this is about? Me being an old high school classmate of Robert's? Really?"

"No. There's more." He was quiet. Too quiet. He pulled over onto the side of the highway, put the car in park, and turned to face me.

My throat dried up like a summer canyon. My shoulders sagged, and my head started to ache. "I don't understand. What are you trying to say?"

"The latest victim ... was Robert's wife. Jazmine Burke is dead."

CHAPTER SEVEN

Friday, December 11

The low rise of the marble stairs curved around an alabaster statue on the third floor. I stood on the first step, looking up at it, mouth open. I shook my head, set my lips back to neutral. The last time I'd passed through this antechamber, I wasn't interested in the priceless works of art. Nick had saved a congressman in a mysterious but heroic way in a distant land that he preferred not to talk about. I had served as Nick's date as he stood before the then-governor to receive accolades and honors. The fish and the dessert were equal parts amazing at the banquet that followed the decoration ceremony.

The vision of a wonderful dinner party sure beat focusing my whirling thoughts on the disaster I'd been drawn into. My eyelids crushed my eyes like anvils and my legs refused to match Nick's long stride. The pain in my shoulder slowed my thoughts, allowing me to savor the anger and fuel my commitment to bringing the killer down.

"I hate to interrupt whatever party's going on in your head, beautiful, but we need to nail down who's playing which role in about thirty seconds." Nick had stopped on the second landing, waiting for me in my sluggish state to catch up.

I started at the sound of his voice. He frowned.

"Looks like someone's a little on the edgy side. This isn't exactly your first rodeo. Why are you so jumpy?" The puzzled look on Nick's face was a rarity.

I smiled, finally joining him on the landing. "Well, it is my first federal case hitting this close to home, and if you must know, I guess I'm a little nervous."

"It's an investigation like any other. You're great at this. Don't over-think. Now, are you going first or am I?" He put his hand on the small of my back and ushered me toward the final flight of stairs.

"Given the way you sped around looking for a parking space, I'd say you should leave the elected officials to me." I stepped ahead of him onto the first marble slab.

"What's that supposed to mean?" He passed me effortlessly, sluicing long legs over the stone risers two at a time and then paused for effect.

"Nick, we're in the state capital. They're gonna be sticklers on laws and stuff. Particularly on breaking them. Like pulling into your not-quite-legal parking spot today."

"I prefer to think of the space as reasonably legal. Besides, I'm FBI. Perks of the job." He reached the top of the stairs and then turned and reached an arm out to me.

The hard marble surfaces of the building echoed with energy as Nick and I strode down the hallway. The door to the governor's office suite was slightly ajar, and sounds of someone talking on a phone drifted through the doorway. We exchanged glances without breaking stride and slid inside. Plush carpet muted our footsteps. Nick waited for the receptionist to end her call before showing her our badges. A moment after she announced our presence over the phone's intercom, she waved us toward the inner office. I pulled open the door. We stood in the doorway while Nick rapped a few times on the wooden doorframe.

Governor Robert Burke leaned over his desk, palms planted on the glossy surface, staring at an open file while murmuring questions to two uniformed men. He looked up and glanced at Nick before locking eyes with me. I gasped at the zap of pain when our eyes met. I held his gaze and nodded subtly. Even in the midst of his private horror, Robert winked at me. Force of habit.

My best friend, Georgi, Robert, Jazmine, and I had been inseparable all four years at Baraboo Senior High School. We'd also been biology lab partners our sophomore year. Dissecting frogs, Georgi and I tossed a coin to see who would make the first incision. Robert made his frog stand up and recite the Gettysburg address to impress Jazmine when the teacher wasn't looking.

After high school, Georgi married Cliff, Robert tied the knot with Jazmine, and we all fell out of touch. After today, I'd still have Georgi and Cliff. But Robert would have non-stop sorrow. Nothing about life was fair.

I was about to learn something beyond horrible based on Robert's expression. He poured over the gruesome crime-scene photos of his wife's murder. The state police hadn't had the sense to deny him his wish to see them. I swooped in, closed the files and pushed them gently toward Nick, all the while keeping my eyes locked on the governor.

My friend didn't say a word as I moved to his side of the desk and hugged him with my good arm. His grief engulfed me, and I sagged as I whispered in his ear, "We'll get this monster, Robert. I promise."

He hugged me harder in response, nodding. We sat down on opposite sides of the desk and spoke in hushed tones. Nick took another leather chair in front of the governor's desk.

"You can say as much or as little as you'd like, Robert. We can get the story from the state team if you've had enough for today." My voice wavered, my eyes moist.

Nick pulled out a notebook and pen. "Anyway you want. If you're more comfortable with just Jo, that's okay too. We're here for you, Governor."

"I hope so. Besides you, Jo is the only one I can stand to talk to right now. So no, I'm good. I have to share this with you, and I want you to know how much it means to me to have you both personally involved."

Nick tensed beside me.

Robert turned intense eyes on Nick. "When Jo Oliver endorses you, that's all the background check I need."

Nick nodded at him.

Smooth move.

"I need to know I have the best men and women working to end this evil, and I know I can trust both of you." He was a shadow of the man I'd supported during the last election. Grief had already taken up residence in him, offering a preview of the havoc it would wreak upon his body, mind, and soul in the coming weeks and months. I needed to relax and absorb every detail he was rational enough to share. I slowed my breathing, quieted my internal dialogue and took out my notebook, sinking into the heavily-padded leather seat. I nodded for him to begin.

"Jazmine volunteered everywhere. You know that, Jo. Everyone knows that. She's been involved in the Mentor Sisters organization since before we were married."

Famous for her passion and poise, Jazmine Burke was one of the most powerful fundraisers in the country. She was the Mentor Sisters' poster child. Had that made her a target for a psychopath?

"Every Saturday morning, she'd bring the girls from Mentor Sisters with her to volunteer at the Farmers' Market on the square. All last summer, they worked with Festers' Flower Farms—you know how she loves her flowers. So, when she decided to volunteer with the girls for the Holiday Fair on the square again this year, I didn't think a thing of it. The glads did it."

"The glads?" Nick looked up from his notebook.

"Gladiolas. She had been working with Drew, her Mentee Sister, selling gladiolas all summer. Drew grew into just as big a flower nut as Jazmine. When Festers decided to freeze-dry some of their best stock and save them for the Holiday Fair, Jazmine and the girl jumped at the chance to turn them into holiday bouquets." His voice trailed off.

I waited for him to continue, moving my gaze past him to the painting of Lake Mendota hanging behind him. If only I was kayaking rather than listening to Robert's sad tale.

"The police report said she'd just sold a big bunch of long-stemmed, purple gladiolas to some dark-haired guy with a walker and she wanted to help him to his car." Robert drew a sharp breath and stared at his hands for several seconds.

My own tears welled up as I pictured the horrible scene and the grisly ending.

"They found the walker knocked on its side next to some gladiolas near the west parking lot. A witness watched her help the guy out of the flower shop, bending over and chatting with him. Gave the police a pretty clear description of the white van she put most of the glads in. He said he didn't give it a second thought. He saw the whole thing—said it happened so, so … normally. He never even knew what he was watching. Never thought to call the cops or report it until his wife saw the story on the news last night. Until Jazmine turned up …"

She'd turned up dead, brutally murdered, skillfully flayed … most likely while still alive. I ached for him. He would have seen every photo, read every description, pieced together a second-by-second understanding of the attack that led to his beautiful wife's death. He was in shock.

Robert and Jazmine had fallen in love in August, right before beginning our sophomore year, in the last seat of a long, yellow school bus. On the ride home from summer camp. Four giant teenage boys had been firing insults at an effeminate boy seated across from them. He asked them to stop after catching an airborne lunch bag with his head. Robert flashed between the bench seats and grabbed the hand of the biggest kid as the first punch was thrown, getting cuffed in the head himself. When I turned back to begin the color commentary with Jazmine, I saw the soft love shining through her tears. They'd been together ever since. How do you get over that?

Robert glided to his feet. Nick and I followed suit. An awkward silence hissed through the room.

"The eyewitness, what happened to him?" Nick was on point. Thankfully.

Robert looked past us. He shifted his weight, clasped his arms around himself, and then unclasped them again. "He's in the hospital right now. Within an hour of the story about him airing on TV, the witness began to receive death threats from all over the state—online and over the phone. Some people are blaming him as if he should've somehow known what was happening and stopped it." He drew in a sharp breath, let it out. "And there was more than a little concern he might harm himself. We don't need any more tragedy to come from this."

I hugged Robert once more before I left the office, Nick in tow.

Our footsteps echoed off the walls, and I shivered at the hollow sounds bouncing around the empty corridors. Snippets of the last moments of Jazmine's life soldered themselves to my subconscious, slowing my steps. Nick reached the end of the grand vestibule. He turned around to watch me as I trod heavily toward him, my eyes tearing up. He nodded as I reached him, and we turned in unison to exit the building.

We paused outside and ducked behind a pillar as he produced a bag of barbeque corn nuts and offered them to me. I tore open the bag and shook several into my palm before handing it back. We descended the steps, passing the bag between us under a canopy of shared silence.

CHAPTER EIGHT

Friday, December 11

"Alright, let's start from the beginning. How many times has this guy struck and for how long? And what do you make of the geography? What's driving him? Are there always little girls involved somehow?" I'd taken the leap and become convinced of all Nick had theorized. This was a consummate killer, and we needed to stop him before he killed again.

"Here's the thing, we think this guy feels right for a ring of unsolved cases centering on the islands, but spanning over a decade."

"What do you mean, 'the islands'? Which islands?" I turned the bag of corn nuts bottom up, shaking the last few morsels and all the crumbs into my mouth.

"Everybody's dream destination. Hawaii." He kept his hands at ten and two on the steering wheel. He could have knocked me over with a feather.

"Hawaii! That's crazy—there's no crime in Hawaii!" I practically screamed the name. A vacation there was near the top of my bucket list. In fact, Del and I were supposed to spend the Christmas holidays at a timeshare in Maui this year. Just a few days from now. Would we still be going?

"And there're no shark attacks there either, right?"

I frowned at Nick's half grin.

"Twelve years ago, a restaurant owner's wife was found dead in the restaurant after hours. She'd been knifed to death.

Death hadn't been quick and hadn't been painless, and there were no signs of drugs at the scene or in her system. That was on Oahu. And she and her husband had just completed the legal adoption of their six-year-old niece, who had been living with them for the past year. The child's biological mother was the suspect from the beginning—messy family case. Three years later—another kill, but this time in Maui."

"Maui?" Maybe there was no safe place on the planet.

Nick filled in as much as he could for me, and even though he held nothing back, the portrait of the killer remained disturbingly elusive. "So basically, every three years, the guy struck again, like clockwork, only on a different island each time. Every murder was unique and had such clear and probable suspects, no one ever made a connection."

Nick moved into the wireless express lane and sped under the toll banner.

"So what happened to connect them? Did something finally pop on ViCAP?"

"Same thing that always happens—he escalated. The twelfth year hit, and instead of choosing a victim every three years, he chose four in one year." We blew by the Illinois state line as he drove. We'd talked nonstop since leaving Madison, and an hour had already flown by.

"There's not a lot to go on." Frustration edged my voice.

"This last victim is what has us convinced of the continued connection." Nick shook his head and stretched as he drove.

"What am I missing?" I clasped both hands and stretched them out before me, yawning.

"One murder of a community volunteer with a heart for the nation's youth is sad. Another murder of a community volunteer who loves working with kids in a different state is alarming, but not enough to connect the dots. A third woman, killed less than four months after the second, known for her work with needy girls in another state? That got our attention."

"You mean it got the attention of the FBI's Violent Criminal Apprehension Program."

"Like I said."

"So, what's the evidence that's firm enough to put ViCAP on alert?"

"First of all, the age and stage of the victims. Thirties to forties, successful, married, well known, and much loved in their respective communities. That, in and of itself, is less common than you'd think. Throw in the fact each of these women volunteered with young girls in some way or another, and each of the kids has been six years old, and you've got yourself a pretty solid victimology. And the timing fits. Every three months, like clockwork. So far."

"Maybe someone who travels for business." I sighed. "Can we stop talking about this for a minute? I'm getting a headache. Pull into the next truck stop so I can get some more barbeque corn nuts, will ya?"

He rolled his eyes and slipped into the right-hand lane, making his way onto the exit ramp. He pulled into a gas station and shut off the car. "All right. But you know the rules. I buy. You fly. And I do mean fly. I want to talk about an exit plan for that violent crime of a marriage you're trapped in, Jo."

His abrupt honesty caught my attention. "I can count the times you've called me Jo on one hand. With one finger."

"I know."

I snapped my head around and looked into his deep-brown eyes. Compassion skimmed the surface as he met my gaze. A tear slipped down my cheek and I glanced away, focusing on opening my door. I looked back at him, offering a small nod and headed into the convenience store.

Fifteen minutes and a tall cup of wretched coffee later, we were back on I-90, southbound for a few miles before turning east toward Haversport, Illinois. And Nick was back on track. "Your marriage is another murder scene waiting to happen.

That's why I can't let this go. It's killing me, watching you let this—let him—slowly squeeze the life out of you. This stops now. I mean it."

"I know."

"Which means what, exactly?"

I sat in stony silence. If only he could read my mind. I didn't want to hide from him, but I didn't want to say the words out loud either. Maybe I could wait him out. I'd managed before.

"Not going anywhere, Josie. You gotta talk this time. You know, use your words, as you're so fond of telling Samantha. Del wouldn't even let you adopt her. Although, why you'd want to subject a child to that sorry excuse for a man is beyond me."

"Look, I don't know what to say without losing the last shred of dignity I have left with you. My marriage is killing me. My husband is killing me. I've got to get out. I know that. There's not a single thing I've done that's made a difference. Things only gets worse. Divorce is the only answer. I know I have to take action, but it's harder than it looks."

This was a lot more than I'd planned on saying. I tore into the bag of corn nuts like my life depended on it. When really, my life depended on getting out of my abusive marriage. I busied myself with the corn nuts and stared out the window, crunching them.

"So what action are you planning, exactly?"

I kept chomping and glaring. "I'm working on it, okay? Things are complicated."

"Waking up in some fleabag motel in Wisconsin Dells with a damaged shoulder and a totaled SUV is complicated too. Way more complicated, in fact. You gotta do something. Now."

"You know we just bought that lakefront property. It's his dream property, and the purchase took every penny of my inheritance, but at least it's keeping him out of my hair. He's spent most of his waking moments over there since the day we closed, and I'm thinking if I can find a way to have him buy me out, maybe I can get a decent settlement and get out fast and cheap."

"Whoa! Are you saying you've already talked to a divorce attorney? I like what I'm hearing."

"No, I ... I've just been thinking a lot about it. It seems there might be a light at the end of the tunnel."

"You gonna keep the old cabin up north?"

"Oh, my gosh! He hates that cabin. I've actually been thinking about doing exactly that, keeping the cabin and fixing it up. It's got great bones. And it would make a great place for a girl to hide from reality once I get myself in gear and this divorce goes viral."

"Once you get going and leave that pig you married, the press is going to have a field day. One bad cop getting the ax from a police chief? This is going to be the best show in town. I'd book it out of town too if I were you."

"Yeah, shut up. I don't want to talk about it anymore."

"Okay, your show, your curtain call. But you know I'm here for you."

I nodded.

"I'll shut up and drive now."

"Finally." I grinned at him.

By the time we turned into my driveway, I'd hatched a plan to call my next-door neighbors and initiate a little weekend getaway at that old cabin in the woods. For them. My own getaway would come. Someday.

After Nick drove away, I unlocked my cell, but my fingers trembled as I punched in their number. A cloud of wistfulness and guilt hovered over me. When Jim and Donna didn't answer, I left a message inviting them to take their own little impromptu holiday road trip up to my cabin. Somebody might as well enjoy it. Given the latest complications of both my personal and professional life, I wouldn't be going up there anytime soon."

CHAPTER NINE

Saturday, December 12

Waking up in my own bed—alone—was like waking up in a foreign land. I stared at the ceiling, wincing as my bruised flesh and torn muscles screamed their own jagged greeting. Images from the crash rolled through my mind. Del's screams, the rushing blur of a tree smashing into the car's front end. I closed my eyes, my heartbeat pounding through my skull. I breathed in deeply, visualizing my heart, willing it to slow down, fill up, relax.

I opened my eyes. Where was Del? What should I do about it? I pulled my phone off my bedside table. Donna and Jim had jumped at the chance to head up to my old cabin on a lark. **We're packed and ready to head to your rustic wonderland any time.**

Crap. It was almost 8:00 a.m. They'd sent the text two hours ago. I texted back.

Go for it amigos. You remember how to get there?

Nick had left two messages. **Call me, beautiful. I'm at the field office. Call your attorney. And your insurance agent.** There was nothing from Del. I checked my email. Silence. Where was he? What was he up to now?

I pushed myself out of bed, grabbed a robe and padded downstairs to make some Jo Java. I like it strong. Real strong. I ground the beans and started the coffee, basking in the aroma. My phone buzzed before the coffee was ready to drink.

Half hour out.

Donna and Jim were making amazing time on their trip to my cabin. Saturday morning traffic was working in their favor. I responded.

Good. You still have the key?

I sipped my first cup of the morning, imagining the short jaunt through Baraboo leading to the old lake road. Next, Donna and Jim would descend Snake Hill and hang a sharp left onto the snow-covered dirt path that went around the lake and right to the door of my cabin. I sure could use that glorious feeling I always got when I turned onto the dirt path that led to my home away from home. At least someone would enjoy a few days of holiday solitude in a beautiful location. I was going to be up to my eyeballs in work. I closed my eyes. Why hadn't I heard from Del? Where had he gone? Who was he with? What was he up to? A dull throbbing settled across both temples.

I poured myself a second cup of coffee. Was Del ever coming home again? His earlier-than-desired resignation from my police department a few years ago had left him embittered and restless. He'd made my life more miserable than usual, blaming me for not fighting harder for him, for not protecting his reputation at work. But how could I? No one knew better than me what that man was capable of. While I had no direct proof that the rumors about missing equipment and inappropriate questioning techniques of witnesses were true, I had no proof that they weren't true either. I'd found a way to remain as neutral as possible. And the blue line wasn't moving. Unfortunately, Del had taken my neutrality as condemnation. Word on the street at the time was that others did too. So far, his job search had not ended well.

I shook my head. Mistake. My temples screamed back at me, a two sledgehammer salute. I texted Nick.

Any news? Meet me at the office and tell me all about it. 10:00 am?

No need to get the folks at the police department riled up about it though.

Scratch that. Meet me at the house.

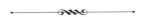

Nick was all business, sporting a regulation black trench coat unbuttoned enough to show off a blue wool suit and red power tie when he rang my doorbell at ten a.m. sharp.

I ushered him in. "What's the other guy look like?"

"He'll speak again, but not above a whisper. I've been at the field office running data since six." He shrugged out of his coat and slung it over the banister. "This guy is slick, but these kills just have to be connected."

"ViCAP pull up anything new?" I led him into the kitchen.

He grabbed a mug from the cabinet, poured himself a cup of coffee and sat down at the counter. "Not really. More scenarios, probabilities. It's still pretty solid, but not conclusive."

"Which means what, exactly?" I topped off my coffee and sat down across from him.

"It's a long shot, but there are a few criminal profiles that are eerily similar to his." His hands were wrapped around his cup.

"Go on." I frowned. He wasn't usually so cagey. Unless he really didn't have much to go on. Sometimes Nick's hunches happened ahead of his evidence—one of the reasons he had a rogue reputation. He couldn't always explain why he knew what he knew. But I'd been around him enough to trust his gut. Was this one of those times?

"Look, the killer, if it is the same guy, has taken three women, in three states, over nine months. We don't know how many other kills he's had, but if this is our guy, we know there likely were others." He stared at me, eyes sparkling.

"Agreed." I sipped my coffee, tapping a finger against the mug.

"And if he's gone from Spokane to Madison, Wisconsin, in the past few months ..." He trailed off, eyes simmering down into a sudden sadness.

"Nick, just because two of the victims are from towns I've had some experience in doesn't mean—"

"I know you don't believe me, but if there's even the slightest possibility you are somehow connected to this guy's psyche, you're in harm's way and I'm not going far until I know for a fact you're in the clear." He had propped his chin up with his fist, looking like a real hot version of *The Thinker.* Lucky me.

"So, what? You're telling me this guy offed one poor woman in LA and another in Spokane because I have family there? And then another in Madison, because I went to high school with the governor? Nick, I love me almost as much as you do, and I'm telling you that's as farfetched as it gets." I hope. Nick lived in these worlds, these murky minds of serial killers, but how in the world would anybody put all of those pieces together? I didn't buy his premise. Strike that. I didn't want to buy it.

But I did buy everything good about this man before me. I smiled at him. And then my smile drained away. A glacier spread over my cheeks. Maybe he was onto something. "Samantha!"

Nick's hand grasped mine. "Relax. She's fine. I called her social worker—William Green, right?—on my way over here. We've got a special agent assigned to her. A female. Undercover childcare worker. Out of an abundance of caution, I've also assigned a protection team to your mother."

"Oh, thank you, thank you." The throbbing in my temples eased to a thrum. I took a deep breath, released it. "So if your idea even is half true, how do we use it to catch this guy?"

"How indeed?" Nick squeezed and released my hand. "That's exactly what we've been pouring over all morning. And right now, I've got more questions than answers."

"Well, that's not exactly terrific news." I rubbed the base of my neck. "Now what?"

Nick got up, drained his coffee and placed the mug in the dishwasher. "You deal with your deadbeat husband on your day off and let me keep following leads back at the ranch."

I slid to my feet, grabbed his coat from the banister and held it out to him. He kissed my forehead. He opened his mouth, but I put my hand up to stop him from talking. "Thank you for being here and for being you. Now go catch that son of Satan and trust me to deal with my marriage."

He looked at me with soulful eyes and turned and walked away.

I spent the rest of the day musing over the many possibilities left in the wake of my husband's absence. By the time I went to bed, I still hadn't made a decision, let alone any phone calls. Without knowing exactly where Del was or what he was planning, I wouldn't make any moves that might force his hand. Yeah, right. I just wasn't in the mood for attorneys. Or anyone else that might hasten the end of my on-again, off-again, marriage.

CHAPTER TEN

Sunday, December 13

After treating myself to coffee and bagels while reviewing the Mentor Sister Serial Killer case notes one more time, I hit the gym. Sunday afternoon was consumed with more ruminating about my marriage and half-hearted attempts to review online information about the murders Nick had referenced. Beyond a film of depression that had wrapped itself around me after learning things I might never unlearn, I had made no real connections. My phone buzzed, and I jumped, but at least the call pulled me out of my funk.

"Dude!" Jim's voice boomed over the miles. "We're doing dinner."

"We are?"

"Yes. You're buying." Jim's smile was as loud as his voice.

"I am?" I was happy to buy, but I wasn't expecting to meet them for dinner.

"Yes. Meet us at the Horse. Right around 5."

Before I could accept or reject his offer, he'd hung up. Well then. I guess I had a dinner date.

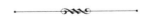

The Rocking Horse Lounge was a shoe-box-sized dive with a wood frame and a green roof, sitting just north of the border between Illinois and Wisconsin. During daylight, the place looked like a Lincoln log house, except for the big white sign propped up by two large telephone poles. The joint served the best burgers in both states and offered an endless supply of chilled beer on tap.

Jim and I both loved the place, but it would mean nothing but agony for Donna, my Fortune 500 CEO friend. With her French-manicured nails and sleek, ivory pashmina, she blended in about as well as a kitten at a committee meeting of the Westminster Kennel Club. Taking pity on her, I tried to hurry Jim through our burgers and beer after filling them in on the smashed car and the latest fight with Del. "C'mon, buddy, drink up. Donna's getting restless."

I picked up my burger and glanced at the sole pool table where a dirty hulk of a guy leaned over the velvety-green slate. Tattoos ringed his left eye. He looked like a biker I had arrested once. Then the guy had the nerve to wink at me. A small, black snake tattoo undulated on his arm when he crouched down to zero in on the cue ball, all the while staring at me.

I fished my badge from my purse and flashed it in Snake Eye's direction so he could get a good glimpse. His expression froze, and then he focused on the cue ball. I snorted and took a big bite out of my burger before turning my attention back to Jim.

His heavy-duty jacket was still zipped up halfway, probably to keep the cigarette smoke from seeping into the loud, blue, Hawaiian shirt he wore. A movie man by trade, Jim owned an impressive collection of authentic Hawaiian shirts. At an even six feet and a hundred eighty pounds of lean muscle, he could actually pull the look off. The combined impact of his costume choices and special effects could tempt you to underestimate him. That would be a mistake.

"Aren't you through yet, honey?" Donna shifted in her chair.

"Hey, don't rush me. A man cannot be hurried through one of the few visceral pleasures of this brief life."

"This is not our final destination, you know. Jo and I want to get home, and we still need to pick up the dogs after we unload tonight, don't forget." Donna retrieved a mirror from her designer bag and freshened up her lip color. The sound of her voice must have charmed him, and he devoured the rest of his burger.

"All right, ladies." He lifted a French fry, dripping with ketchup. "A toast to the most excellent adventure of the past forty-eight hours at Jo's most excellent cabin in the woods. And to think, I spent dinner with the two most beautiful blondes north of the border." Jim stuffed the fry in his mouth and winked at his wife.

Donna rolled her eyes. "He's incorrigible."

A trickle of laughter snuck out of the side of my mouth. The hint of a smile broke through and within a few seconds, I was laughing full bore. Jim put his hand in the air, and we bumped fists victoriously, his dark-brown eyes full of mirth. I slapped my hand into his and when we stood up, he pulled me to him, crushing me into a bear hug.

"First step is the hardest, Jo. The rest will come faster than you think. You can do better. You're gorgeous, you're brilliant, and you're the chief of police. It doesn't get any hotter than that."

He kissed me on the forehead and pulled away. In one swift motion, he linked arms with Donna and me, carting us out the door with him into the chilly evening.

Donna rode with me so we could continue talking about Del as we drove through the dark, winding streets on our way home. How much of her lively banter had been tailor-made for me, my gift from an unseen God wrapping me securely in a blanket of comfort and warmth? I needed warmth and security now more than ever. Having two such wonderful neighbors was a sweet gift.

I entered the back of our subdivision, passing the large, Christmas-bedecked homes of friends and neighbors. I turned onto our block and both of our houses came into view.

"Josie?" Donna muttered.

I eased my foot off the gas, dialing down the rest of the evening into slow motion. There was my house—lit up like a Christmas tree. Bright light spilled out into the street, reflecting off the snow and back onto the house. Every light was on, everything so very wrong. Stripped walls showed through undressed windows. Security spotlights focused on empty areas through the windows of my once beautiful home.

What had happened? The front door stood wide open. Both garage doors were up. Litter blew haphazardly across the yard. Footprints, car tracks, and truck tracks crisscrossed the driveway, spilling onto the lawn. The depth of the tracks and the width of the tires indicated a large, heavy vehicle had been parked in the yard at some point over the last few hours. Deep ruts branded the snow-covered lawn on the side of the porch. Something hefty had been dragged across my front yard.

The gurgle of water running somewhere grew louder as I parked my pickup truck in the driveway. Jim parked their car in their driveway a few feet away.

We stepped out of the warm truck and stared at the desolate scene. I started toward the house flanked by Donna and Jim. Together, we trudged up the front steps of my home like complete strangers. The ornate iron mat was missing from the top of the porch steps. I had nailed the mat into place with my brand new nail gun two weeks after settling into our new home, nine years ago. It must have taken some work to pull it up.

We followed muddy footprints to the front door and paused, glancing at each other nervously. Two small pine trees were missing from the concrete urns by the door. One of the urns was missing too. My house lay barren.

The large front windows offered a detailed view of the chaos within. My holiday decorations had been completely destroyed, festive strands of tiny white lights ripped down, cords left dangling. I could not force myself to move.

Jim swore, and Donna spoke into my ear, but I couldn't understand a thing they were saying. Donna steadied herself with a hand against the cedar siding, and we huddled in the doorway like uninvited guests.

The entryway and stairwell walls were bare except for black kick marks, and worse, they'd been punched in spots, drywall pushed in all the way to form dark holes. I moved inside to the powder room off the foyer and would have fainted if not for the warmth of Donna's welcome presence at my side.

I stumbled into my kitchen and had to hold on to the wall to keep from dropping to my knees. This was not my kitchen. Muddy scars marred the once-gleaming hardwood floors. Every cupboard had been torn open and ransacked. Some of the cabinet doors had been ripped off the hinges. One of them was completely missing. Another lay broken on the rug by the back porch door. A mad, hungry giant had violated and defiled my home, had ripped everything away from its careful place in my world.

I stood in the remains of my kitchen, dizzy, unable to think. The mottled surface of my island countertop was scratched and smeared with smudgy prints. A cream-colored piece of paper rested at the edge of the counter, a page torn from one of my journals. Leaning against the counter, I read the note left behind by my husband.

> Jo: I've just filed for divorce. I have another woman and a very good attorney. Our relationship ended four years ago when you and the thin blue line betrayed me. Ours is a business arrangement that has come to an end, and it's time to divide the

assets. You need to get an attorney. Know this: I want the lake-front property and everything I took with me today. And the boat, my share of hard cash, and all the vehicles. If you don't fight me on this, I will leave you alone. If you do fight me, I'll go for everything you have or ever hope to have. Don't fight me. You can't win.—Del

I reached for my work phone to make the call that would change my life forever.

CHAPTER ELEVEN

Sunday, December 13

I punched in the number and squeezed my eyes shut. I didn't breathe until the ringing stopped, and then I growled as Nick's voicemail droned on. I opened my eyes and spoke into the phone. "Nick, I need you. Now."

My second and last call of the evening went to my Deputy Chief, Lauren Mitchell—Mitch. She was a natural leader, and I had known I was going to elevate her to my second in command before my first official day on the job. I'm good that way. I can read people. Most people that is, except for the ones I marry.

Cop to the core, she answered on the first ring despite the fact it was eight p.m. and she should've been relaxing with her family.

"Chief?" Her groggy voice held promise—a lifesaver tossed straight to me in the midst of the rocky waves of my new reality. I could picture her dark red hair mussed from napping on the couch in front of a TV movie. Her husband of three years softly snored in the background. They were just starting out, and everything I saw between them was everything I wanted.

The picture brought me to tears. "Mitch, I have a personal emergency to tend to. Del left me ... for good, I think."

Breathless, every word constricted, I read the note to her, and then I choked out a mini version of the hell I had entered.

"Chief! Do you need me to come over? What can I—"

"Would you please shut up? That's all I've got right now. Look, I gotta go."

"Oh, my gosh! I'm so, so sorry." Her voice was low, and she spoke in measured tones after listening to my ice-cold explanation of events over the phone. "What do you need most from me right now?"

My stomach tightened. I drew a sharp breath and wiggled my mouth to loosen up the muscles of my jaw enough to respond to her. Donna and Jim stood with their backs to me in front of the fireplace, whispering in low tones as they surveyed the damage in what used to be my great room. I turned away from them.

"I need you to be me. I need you to go into my office in the morning, business as usual. I need you to run the show for me, buy me some time. Just sit in my chair and stay there for the next twenty-four hours, okay?"

"No. Nothing's okay. There is nothing at all okay about any of this. I'm on my way."

"Mitch! Just sit tight for right now. Can you do that for me?"

"I got your back, Chief. Any time, any place. You just hang in there, and call me when you need me. Anything else?"

"Nope—just thanks, Mitch. Later." I ended the call, my hands still shaking.

Thirty minutes later, Nick stood by my side, and we walked through the remains of my home together. I laughed at the five-hundred-dollar pair of Italian loafers he'd pulled on bare feet under his favorite pair of jeans with a white button-down shirt. His clean silhouette was in stark contrast to the chaos all around us as I slogged through every room on my second tour that evening. I stopped short on the upstairs landing and waved Nick forward. I let him take in the emptied bedroom scenes alone. I didn't need to see those again right then. He swore as he padded softly down the stained, carpeted stairs.

"That pig is going to pay for it this time, Josie." He pulled his phone out of his shirt pocket, opened the notebook app and sat down on the stairs beside me. "Del cannot get away with this! And who lives in a neighborhood that lets this kind of stuff go on without callin' the cops! Where is everyone?"

"Think about it, Nick. It's almost Christmas. We're about the only two families in the subdivision not hiding out on some tropical island. Place is as good as deserted this time of year."

"And, of course, Del would know that. You're gonna be so much better off without him. You know that, don't you?"

Tears flowed down my cheeks, and my throat swelled so tight that all I could muster was a hoarse whisper. "I don't know. I just don't know anything anymore." Steel knots roiled in my belly, and I started seeing stars. "Look, I'm not okay right now. I need some time to pull myself together—to figure all this out. I need you to go home and be your amazing, professional self so I can fall apart. I need some time to see exactly what I'm up against. Might take a little ride out to the lake-front property. We'll see what I need to do next."

My voice cracked. I was skating on the bitter edge.

"You know I'm here for you, right? But, listen. I have to know you aren't going to be alone. Can I stop by later? Can I send Mitch over? Maybe make this one official?"

"No, honey. That ain't how this is gonna work. I can't deal with that right now. I just need you to step in come daylight. Keep the serial killer investigation hot, do your best without me for a few days, and don't call me unless you really need me. You're the only one I want to hear from, so make sure any case updates go through you. I am not in the mood for anything or anyone else today."

"Sure. I'll step away and have your back. But you're not going through this alone. I don't care how tough you are."

"Fair enough. I'll stay with Donna and Jim, so relax. And I mean it. Other than you and them, I really don't want to see anyone. I sure can't talk about this officially yet. I've got to think things through. That day has come though, trust me. I will make this one official, and we will drag his sorry butt in."

"All right, I'll take off then. And I'll make sure Mitch checks in with you after the six a.m. roll call. And, Josie? I'm here for you. Whatever you need." He stepped into my space until only a whisper stood between us. The air came alive with the heat that rolled off his body onto mine. He lowered his voice to husky. "Josie, I'm here for you. Always have been, always will be."

A crooked grin crept across my face. Who was this man? How'd I get so lucky? "Thanks. I'll keep you posted."

He wrapped his arms around me, kissed the top of my head, and held me for several seconds before pulling away. I looked up at him with moist eyes and watched him trail slowly down the stairs. Once he vanished through the broken front door, I used my shirtsleeve to wipe the tears from my face.

But my tears had only just begun.

CHAPTER TWELVE

Monday, December 14

"Hi, sweetie, ready for some coffee?" Donna's voice woke me as she breezed into her guest bedroom with two steaming mugs, dressed to the nines for work. It was already seven a.m. Monday morning. Jim would be long gone by now. I hadn't heard a thing since crashing at their place a few hours ago.

Monday. Wow. Harsh reality, and I just wasn't ready for it. Donna pushed the covers aside and sat lightly on the bed. I eased up and we drank in silence. She took my hand and squeezed.

"Donna, what happened? He's gone, and he's trying to crush me on the way out. What did I do to deserve this? How could he? How long has he been planning this?" Sobs surged forth, and I was right back on the edge of out-of-control. "And by the way, this in the middle of the worst case I've ever had the bad sense to get caught up in. I don't know which is worse—my professional life or my personal life. It's one giant nightmare all rolled into one."

"That's it. I'm staying home with you today." Donna tipped her cup up and drained it. I put my mug on the bedside table, strong objections standing at attention on my tongue, but she kept right on talking. "Resistance is futile. I'm staying with you. I don't want you to be alone right now. We'll face this day together."

Her kindness was met by my silence, even though I really, really wanted nothing more than to cry for a week. Maybe two. My head hurt so badly, I could barely think. "Thank you. I don't even know what to do first. But I'm pretty sure I couldn't get to it without you carping at me all day long."

"It's what we do. We do for each other. I'm here for you. Now, shut up and get some rest."

"Yes, ma'am. But could you at least allow me the courtesy of my one phone call?"

She smiled, triumphant, produced my phone out of her suit pocket and slipped out the door.

Silence filled the room. I had the luxury of facing my personal hell undistracted for a few minutes, surrounded at a distance by my loving friends—half of whom were definitely well armed, locked, and loaded. A glimmer of gratitude pierced the blackness in my mind. I'd been lucky, even blessed, in the midst of this miserable moment.

I poured over my calendar, and I reviewed what I could recall of this week's agenda at the police department. There were two personnel issues Mitch could handle easily, along with a scheduled department skills assessment at the shooting range she could run without me. I had room to breathe, and I was pretty fortunate to be in my fourth year as chief of police in Haversport instead of in my first chaotic year. I'd had the opportunity to put a fine crew in place over the years. Most of my officers were self-sufficient—well equipped to handle any emergency. More or less.

Nick was following up a lead on our serial killer this morning, and I would let him handle the investigation for now. He wanted me to call a divorce lawyer today. There was no big news afoot in our boring little village. No nasty criminals needed to be captured or killed. No ne'er-do-wells on the edge or even seeking refuge at our shiny new station. No dangerous, deadbeat spouses on the lam—except for mine. All in all, not a bad place to be when facing what I was facing. At least my professional world was holding its own while my personal life tanked.

Deep thoughts for my first cup of coffee. I crawled my way out of bed. Donna had laid out some jeans for me. She must've gone through my clothes next door. God bless her. Hers would never fit me. She was shapely and petite. My curves were rounder, and all five-foot-seven of me hung from an athletic frame.

The warmth of a shower spurred me back to life as I played over the events of last night one more time. My mind wandered down the empty hallways and the broken plaster of my home. The one question I couldn't stop asking myself— who is she?—hung just beyond my reach, overshadowed by an equally ominous question. How much worse was this all going to get?

I stepped out of the shower and dried off with a plush white towel. I examined myself in the mirror. Which parts of me hadn't pleased my husband? What sort of body had replaced mine? Heaviness crushed me, pushing me off balance, and I sank to the toilet seat, clutching the thick towel around me. Could I even go on? Did I even want to?

I got up and dressed.

I headed downstairs to the kitchen. Donna sat in front of the hearth, waiting for me. I plopped into an overstuffed chair next to her.

"How did this latest horror start? What happened, Jo?"

"There's nothing to tell that you don't already know."

"Did something happen recently that threw him over the edge?"

My heart beat wildly. Red heat rocketed up the small of my back toward my face. My throat tightened, and I tried to keep the venom out of my voice. "Donna, I'm telling you, I didn't do a thing. He's the bad guy here. I told you he tried to kill me with his car, and the whole time he had a girlfriend on the side. If he thinks he's gonna take away our dream lake property, he better have his head examined. I'm taking a road trip out there. Now."

"Do you think that's wise?"

"I'm going. I have to, and I'm going alone."

CHAPTER THIRTEEN

Monday, December 14

Driving always calmed me, and my pickup truck would get me to the lake and back safe and sound. I'd worry about sane later. The Bluetooth chirped. I pressed the little telephone icon on the steering wheel and said hello into thin air.

"Come get me, beautiful." Nick's smooth tones filled the truck.

"Nick!"

"Donna texted me, so just come get me. I've got everything you need, sweetener and all. I'm at the corner of Hainesville and 120. Keeping it hot, just the way you like it."

I was grinning like a schoolgirl by the time we finished the call. Leave it to Donna to have my back. I had company on the ride into the unknown after all. Three minutes later, I pulled into the parking lot where he was waiting for me in his nondescript, government-issue, dark sedan. As soon as he pulled his sleek frame out of the front seat, I could focus on nothing but him. He glided over to my side of the truck. I lowered the window and smiled at him as he set the coffee down on the pickup's hood.

"Hey, beautiful." He leaned into my window and gave me a quick kiss on the cheek. Placing his hand on the door, he offered me the coffee life saver.

"Cut the foreplay and get in." I gave him my best cop glare, and he shook his head, laughing. He moved around the front of the truck and slid into the passenger seat.

"You know you want me, Josie. Just a matter of time. No worries. I can wait a little longer. Gonna be worth it. Gonna definitely be worth it." He reached for my hair, swirling a lock around those perfectly formed fingers.

"At least someone's in a good mood today."

I kept the faux hardness in my voice, but my emotions were on overdrive. Energy sparked between us as Nick informed me the lead had not panned out. Then he regaled me with current FBI cases in other places. His chatter was strangely comforting. Still, as we followed the familiar route west on 120 toward the lake house—my husband's dream house—I fell apart in silence. Nick's hand moved to my shoulder as I drove. I had the presence of mind to switch off the Bluetooth before calling Mitch along the way. I owed it to her to catch her up, and even though I'd filled her in on the basics last night, I poured out the full version of my sad marriage tale to her. I glanced over at Nick, and his face looked grim and angry as he learned even more than I'd previously told him about Del's abuse.

Mitch's little saltbox of an office must've been shaking from the rafters at the news. She stayed calm, cool, and collected, though. And for the hundredth time in the last twenty-four hours, I wondered if everyone but me had seen this coming. No one else seemed all that surprised at my horror show.

"I'm sorry, Mitch. This is all so unbelievable, I can't take it all in. I don't know what to say."

"This is a horrible way for your marriage to end. But in a way, he's done you a favor. There's no decision to agonize over any more. He left you. It's out of your hands. Wait a minute ... I hear traffic noise. Are you driving somewhere right now?"

"Take a breath, Mitch. Yes, I'm in a car, but Nick's by my side. I need to check on the lake house."

"Don't do this to yourself. You don't know what he's capable of. Turn back. Please."

"I have to do this. I love you. I don't know what else to say. I'll call you. Gotta go." I ended the call, and Nick came alive.

"What'd she say about us going out there?"

"Very bad idea."

"And you said?"

"We're practically there."

"Great."

I hadn't noticed slowing down during my chat with Mitch, but the speedometer was hovering around fifty now. I slammed my foot on the gas, and the truck accelerated to over seventy. One more light, a left turn, and a country road would bring us face-to-face with the lake house. Numb, I sped through the light and then sat back in the deep, leather seat, preparing myself for the unknown.

The house sat back quite a way from the road—the only thing it had in common with my little cabin in Baraboo, Wisconsin. Twin brick towers marked the driveway, complete with lanterns. We pulled in, sailed around the circular drive, and parked in front of the three-car garage. The roof over the middle stall was peaked, specially built for boat storage and complete with a porthole-like window in the center of the dormer. I entered the garage door code for the middle door.

Nick touched my arm. "Josie ..."

I followed his gaze to the snow-covered gravel path leading to the custom-built boat house edging the pristine lake below. Parked on the pathway next to the boathouse were two identical haul-it-yourself trucks. Thick layers of frost covered the windshields of both vehicles. A low fog crept up from the ground and slowly washed over me as I gazed at the trucks. The fog wisped through my mind, carrying a swirling mass of images of Del and another woman. I willed the images away but they stood their ground, beating together like an out-of-control Mixmaster. I shook my head, blinked back tears. Who was she?

In unison, we turned back to the garage—eerily bare—no boxes, no vehicles. A different sight than the one on my last visit. Del and I had spent the previous weekend here. I had painted and wallpapered rooms, playing out my ideas on our new home. I had spent a small fortune on custom fabrics, papers, and linens. Doing the work myself was one of my concessions to Del's concerns about spending so much so soon.

Nick took my arm as we walked through the garage. It was too quiet. I unlocked the door and stepped into the kitchen.

My gaze rested on the custom-built kitchen table. Del and I had taken my mother to an Amish colony in Wisconsin this past summer to commission the table and chair set. I'd known the man who built this table since high school. Sitting on the middle of my table was a feminine-looking basket that was not mine surrounded by giftwrap. Gaily colored ribbons and a card sat on a Bible next to it—opened to a passage about forgiveness. The note was to my husband. From another woman.

Every detail of the scene was meticulously frozen and stored in separate compartments in my mind, to be scrutinized in the upcoming days, weeks, and months. There were two coffee mugs in my sink. One of the cups was stained with bright-red lipstick, hardly smudged, as if the lip print had been painted on. I picked up the mug and turned it around in my shaking hands to get a good look at the impression on the rim. This revolting evidence jarred me, and the mug fell out of my hand into the sink below, snapping the handle off cleanly.

My heart seized, my lungs stung, and I sucked in air as white-and-black pinpricks flashed before me. I screamed. Then I screamed again, louder. I picked up the stained and broken mug and flung it against the granite floor. The crashing ceramic shattering against the stones lit an inner fuse. I picked up one of the shards, slammed it back onto the floor, and stomped on it, screaming all the while. My throat was burning. I stopped screaming, raised my face to the ceiling and took several deep breaths. I closed my eyes, slowly letting out the last breath. Then I opened my eyes and gave Nick a weak smile. He put his arms around me, and I stood silently, staring at the shattered mug.

We walked down the hall to the unfinished powder room. Someone had moved my hand-painted wooden sign. In its place jeered a plastic-coated, eight-by-ten-inch picture of Del looking drunken and seedy, smiling in a way I'd never seen him smile before. Another woman had placed a photo of my husband on my wall in my unfinished powder room. My stomach roiled.

We followed the hallway into the office. Brown-paper grocery bags sat on the desk. A pair of my favorite riding jeans spilled over the top of one of the bags. I'd moved some of my clothes over a few weeks earlier in anticipation of living here full time as soon as our other house had sold. I stepped forward, touched the fabric, and froze in place. Could I feel his presence, or hers?

Nick waited for me to lead the way to the master suite. A dresser stood out from the wall opposite the bed. I went through each drawer. The bottom drawer held a woman's clothes, lingerie, candles, and a trashy DVD. I started swimming in nausea, and I must have doubled over.

Nick came to my side. "Let's go, Josie. Enough. We've seen way too much already today."

I ignored him and stepped into the walk-in closet. Del had placed my blouses in a paper sack. My evening bags lay haphazardly on the floor. Some other woman's shoes sat next to Del's. Backless, gold, faux-leather with four-inch heels.

I ran to the bathroom and went through every drawer in his vanity, finding condoms on two different shelves. In my own cabinets, a fragrance I didn't use. My monogrammed hand towels lay damp and crumpled on the counter. A pair of panty hose bunched up against the bottom of the cabinet.

I walked out of the bathroom, down the hall, and into the great room. I sank to my knees before the spotless wall of windows. A row of pine trees swayed in the wind. I used to think those pines beckoned me to the lake. Nick joined me without a sound.

Del and I had fought for months about buying this brand-new, oversized luxury home for just the two of us. Finally, my hefty inheritance from a recently deceased aunt, and Del's accusation that I'd never let him have his dream, won out. I had plunked down nearly every penny I had in an effort to save our marriage by giving Del exactly what he said he needed to be happy.

"Turns out 'happy' doesn't last very long." Given Nick's solemn look, I'd finished my thought out loud.

I moved my knees under me and grunted to my feet. Now it was crystal clear how badly that SOB had manipulated me.

It would be satisfying to catch him in the act with his mystery woman and shoot him in the head. But what good would that do me? Better to see him brought to justice. If there was any justice for what he'd pulled. Probably not. Letting him live and pursuing justice would end up costing me a lot more in the long run than him good and dead. And his little "friend" too.

The saxophone tones of my work cell yanked me out of my dark reveries. "Yeah."

"Chief Oliver?"

"Frank?"

"Yeah, it's me. And this isn't a social call. Where are you?"

"Ah, out at the lake house with a buddy, why?"

Silence. "Is that the best place for you to be right now?"

"Sir?"

"Just ... look. I need you to drive in. Now. Get out of there. That's not the smartest place in the world for you to be or be seen today."

"Okay, Sheriff. Mind telling me why?"

"I want to make sure we get ahead of the storm before the bottom drops out." Chills crept up the back of my neck, and the pinch of a headache worked its way up to my temples.

"Storm, sir?"

"The storm that Del created. What, you didn't think I'd hear? It's everywhere already. And it's ... complicated. Come in, and we'll talk."

He hung up, and I stared at the phone as if it were alive. I snuck a look at Nick. He was gazing at me, waiting for my direction. The sound of tires on gravel turned our heads. A caterer's van drove past the house, heading down to the water where several other majestic homes lined the lake.

I sighed. "Let's go. I was hoping to poke around the boathouse, but that's going to wait for another day. I don't want to watch new neighbors happily prepping for a holiday party I haven't been invited to. I've seen enough for one day. Not that I've much of a choice in the matter anyway. That was the sheriff. He wants to get a handle on the PR nightmare my life has become. I'll come back later."

I opened the door to the garage, and Nick and I descended the four steps single file. He had been a rock, and he hadn't gone ballistic when he saw what Del had done. We pressed on through the expansive garage and reached the truck. He held open his hand and I tossed him the keys without question.

"We'll come back later." I said again with a tight smile as he backed the truck into a y-turn and nosed slowly down the drive.

I turned around in the seat for a few seconds, watching the little shed down the hill recede through the back window. The caterer's van had vanished around the bend. I pulled my eyes away and watched the ground lining the driveway. Bulbs I'd planted in the fall flanked the drive and surrounded both brick pillars. In a few months, they'd be in full beauty. Where would I be by then?

CHAPTER FOURTEEN

Monday, December 14

Nick pulled into the coffee shop where we had left his car and hurried inside. He emerged in record time, with two familiar cups of heaven.

"This gonna be enough to tide you over on the way home, beautiful?" He leaned in and handed me the cup.

"You're a life saver, Nick. In every way." I smiled my thanks and he nodded at me, winked and turned on his heel. By the time I got home, there were three trucks and one sedan parked in my driveway. Donna descended from my front porch and waved me over. I rolled down the window. "Donna?"

She didn't say anything, but the ghost of a smile pulled across her face, and she stepped close. "You know how I love to decorate. Thought you could use a little help."

My head dropped forward and my eyes grew wide as I looked from her to my driveway. She waved a hand at me and nodded her head as if to tell me to get out of my truck. I stepped out into the cold air.

"When did you have time to do all this, and wait, is that Mitch's car?"

"Could be. I'd go see what the fuss is about if I were you. Now scoot!"

I walked between the two trucks, nodding at the local handyman behind the wheel of the white van. Mitch smiled at me from her village-issue police town car and rolled the window down at my approach. She held out a cup of coffee and tilted her head at the passenger door. I laughed as I trotted over and plunked into the warm seat.

We drank in silence for a few moments. I was watching the workers when Donna walked up to my side of the car. I rolled down the window to talk to her.

Donna leaned in. "You go ahead and do whatever it is you ladies do in the name of the law. Ms. Mitchell will take you to the office. I'll spend the day with these lovely workmen and see what we can do about some home improvements."

"And all that stuff about agreeing with me not going to work today?"

"Oh, that. Yeah, well, that might've been a bit of a ruse to occupy us long enough for Jim to set this enterprise in motion. I knew you'd want to go and 'man up,' as you say, around your office yet today. Am I right?"

I jumped out of the car, hugged her tightly, and whispered, "Thank you, Donna."

She hugged me back before turning me toward the car. I raised my hand in thanks as Mitch maneuvered the car around on my ice-covered lawn and made her way to the street.

"What kind of barbarian driving is this?"

"First things first." She raised her coffee cup in a silent salute and drove on.

I nodded. "You know something?"

"Nope. Enlighten me."

"I think I'm gonna survive this mess. I really do."

"That's my girl!" She drove out onto the slick street and stepped on the gas, eliciting warning beeps as the car fishtailed on the ice, and we laughed out loud again.

Mitch reached behind my seat. She pulled out her dress-blues' hat and placed it on my head. I was still laughing when I reached out to bump fists with her. I pulled down the visor and played around in the mirror.

"Halfway home, girl. Having a good hair day and a great hat day. Now we'll just have to see about the rest. I gotcha covered." Mitch pointed to the back seat.

I turned around and smiled at one of my dress uniforms, still wrapped from the last trip to the dry cleaners. A favorite pair of calfskin designer pumps sat on the seat next to the newly emptied hat bag. "I owe you one."

"Yup."

Our next stop was Mitch's house. Her husband met us at the door and gave me one of his soul-cleansing hugs. Their presence radiated peace—hope even. Mitch opened the powder room door and hung my uniform on a hook. They were quietly talking as I closed the door to change.

Mitch's fabulous foresight and attention to detail had led her to choose my favorite navy-blue wool work skirt. I'd had this uniform carefully tailored until it showcased my five feet seven inches to maximum advantage. I'd need every little perk I could find to force myself back into my work routine today.

I was also having a fantastic hair day, courtesy of Donna's salon-quality equipment. I'd taken the time to blow out my dark-blonde hair into the straight and silky style reflected in the vanity's mirror. I never left my bedroom without performing my basic skincare routine, donning gold jewelry, and spritzing on a favorite fragrance. At least, I still had my morning ritual working for me—with a little help from my friends today. All in all, not a bad look despite the tired eyes, tear-stained face, and doomed-to-all-get-out new life.

I opened the door and stepped into the foyer, ready for anything. Mitch waited with two travel cups of coffee. She handed me a mug, nodding slightly. I accepted it with a shrug. The aroma alone was enough to send me into a caffeine high.

"Let's roll," she said as she pulled open the front door.

The richness of the coffee and the bond between us were all we needed as we sailed through the streets in companionable silence.

We were pulling into her parking spot at the police station when she turned to me. "Chief? You thinking about an attorney yet?"

"Not yet."

"You have to. The sooner the better. You need to get a good lawyer, and you need to start making some contacts today. You want me to get on it for you? Call around, make some inquiries?"

"No. Thanks, though. I get it. I know I need to start moving, and I'll get there soon. I may need you when the time comes. Until then, let's just walk through that door and get 'er done."

"Roger that, Chief."

Mitch and I climbed the stone steps and stood at the back door of the station.

"You sure you're up for this?"

"Yeah, I'm up for it. All I'm gonna do is sneak in, stomp around and let everyone know I'm alive and well. Perfect timing. Most of 'em should be at lunch by now."

"Good point. So, we doin' this thing?"

"On three." I adjusted the hat on my head.

We opened the door into a stairwell. Mitch headed downstairs to the shooting range, and I headed up to my office. With any luck, it'd be deserted at noon on a Monday. I pushed the fire door open and stepped into a hallway with black-and-white diamond linoleum. The hall wound past storage lockers, a utility room, and a break room, before turning into a smaller, carpeted hallway. Tiny offices hugged both sides for about twenty feet. A large open area, containing the call center and computer surveillance and conference rooms, stood at the end of the hallway. There were three corridors leading out of the open area, and I took the first right. My receptionist was at her desk in the center of the hallway. Our eyes met as I walked across the soft carpet.

"Afternoon, Chief. Are you here for your meeting?" This was Liz-speak for "I got your back, Chief." Her way of telling me she knew everything that had happened in the past twenty-four hours.

"Yeah, hold my calls," I mumbled as I swept past her, shutting the door louder than I'd intended. I wasn't being fair to her, but I couldn't handle our usual banter this afternoon. And I sure didn't have it in me to talk about my ridiculous new lack of a life. Tragedy or comedy? Who knew?

It was all I could do to walk into the building with Mitch like we'd done every day for the past four years, and I was hoping to keep my personal crisis close to the vest. Until I ran into Liz.

She'd been my faithful assistant and number-one fan every minute of every day since I took the position of chief of police. And she was everyone's ideal woman. Youthful radiance and healthy blonde hair framed cornflower-blue eyes set perfectly into an unforgettably beautiful face. Half the guys in the department were speechless around her. The other half constantly vied for her attention. But Liz was simply Liz—sweet, professional, happily married, and holding us all together day in and day out. She'd no doubt been under Mitch's influence already today. Given my stellar impersonal performance, she'd probably even sent an emergency text message, tattling on me to Mitch.

Whatever. I let my breath out in a long, low stream, bracing myself against the office door for a second. What was I doing here today? Oh, yeah, Sheriff Frank wanted me here. But I needed to be here for me. To have a place to call my own, to keep my world spinning, to get back to my normal life. Guess it wasn't working all that well so far.

Two raps sounded on the door. "Chief? Can I come in?"

"Yes, of course. C'mon in, Liz."

"I just wanted to let you know I'm here for you—if you need anything." She stepped up to my desk as she appraised me. What did she think of my formal attire, fabulous hair, and the deepening bags under my eyes? I should've known she'd be way ahead of me. "I'm so glad you're here for the holiday party. Commander Mitchell would have done a fine job, but it's you everyone really wants to see. I know you'll be your amazing self, and the families will appreciate your personal attention." And in one smooth motion, Liz pulled me back into my work world. I'd forgotten all about today's party. Liz had her notebook out and was bound to get me caught up. So I tuned in.

"So far, nothing unusual has come up. I was here for the six o'clock report this morning. York called in sick. Again. I already asked Hernandez to check him out. Probably not legit, but doubt we'll be able to prove it, again." She flipped a page. "And you didn't miss much last week. Just the usual, not-so-happy holiday domestic calls. Nothing you haven't seen before. All handled by Commander Mitchell. We do still have that three o'clock meeting scheduled to review the personnel investigation results with the mayor. I've already heard from him that he'd be happy to reschedule."

I looked up into Liz's clear-blue eyes, catching the hint of a nod. Her way of telling me the mayor knew about my personal nightmare. And if he knew, everybody knew.

"No, let's keep it. Thanks. And the ceremony's at what, six?"

"Actually, we have it set for four-thirty tomorrow over at the Paradise County College conference room."

"What? Why are we at the PCC? I hate that conference room."

"Because it's the middle of winter, and it's the only place that will hold the ceremony unless you want to go back to the courthouse. Do you not remember having this conversation last week?"

"Oh, yeah. It's all coming back to me now. Thanks. Anything else I should know about or remember?" I winked at her and moved around the desk, letting her know we were back to being on the same side again. She was nervous, and I wanted to reach out to her as she'd reached out to me.

She shifted her gaze downward and fidgeted for a moment before she spoke again. "Well, nothing more for today. But you were scheduled to be out of town starting on Wednesday, you know."

I gasped and sat down hard on the edge of my desk. My stomach roiled. My head started pounding. Del and I had planned on spending the holidays at our timeshare in Maui. We were set to leave on Wednesday for two weeks in paradise. Some paradise. "Yeah, about that."

"I'm just so sorry!" She set her notebook on my desk and clasped my hands in both of hers as tears spilled down her cheeks.

"I can't do this right now, Liz. Please … leave me alone … just for now, okay?"

She nodded, retrieved her notebook, and stepped out of my office. I sat on the side of my desk for a very long time, watching the shadows grow longer in the afternoon sunlight.

Then I rallied, and spent the next few hours reviewing case notes on the Mentor Sister Serial Killer. Nick was following up on Jazmine's murder, and we both feared the killer would strike again. But he wanted me to take some time before leaping back into the case. I tried to release my mind to sift through the notes and make connections, but it wasn't working. And every time I thought about the once-vibrant women dying so horribly, an overwhelming darkness spread through me, rendering me nearly powerless. All I wanted to do was stop. Stop being. Stop doing. Stop existing.

Force-feeding myself happier scenes, I wandered into memories of my first ride on my horse, Max, and the exhilaration of winning our first equestrian event together. But Del had been there, and scenes stretched out and included him against my will. I must stop thinking about Del, but that made it impossible to think about anything else.

The texture of his leather jacket under my eager hands as he tore through mountain passes on his Harley, our bodies shifting and leaning in unison as he navigated switchbacks and narrow roads on our way to the top. The devil-take-all plunge on the way down in the moonlight, my happy screams bursting forth at every surprise in the road on our way toward forever together. The brevity of the mountain top experience we'd shared but could not sustain, no matter how hard I scraped and clung and scaled. A pinnacle reached that could not keep me from the unrelenting nose-dive down the other side.

Darkness enveloped me like mist over a riverbed, and my whole body seemed foreign and depleted. I tried to think of happy memories or objects to ward off the pull of this cauldron of emotions, but all I could find was a deepening sense of hopelessness, with a burgeoning side of self-hatred.

Where was this coming from? Maybe I should see a psychiatrist. But who? And how to describe this despondency? I closed my eyes and envisioned a red briefcase with a brass clasp and matching hinges. I visualized picking up the dark thoughts by the scruff of the neck and placing each one in the smooth, leather briefcase. Then I snapped it shut and locked it tight.

I had to pull it together for that afternoon's dreaded meeting. One of our finest had been accused of being a little heavy-handed with the jail's "overnight guests," and I was scheduled to share a summary of investigation results as well as my recommendations with the village leadership team.

As much as I wasn't looking forward to the confirmation of inappropriate behavior I was about to deliver about a member of my staff, at least I finally had to face some bad news that wasn't my own. Beat the stuffing out of the chat I'd have to have later with the sheriff.

The meeting went off without a hitch. The most notable aspect was how difficult it seemed for the three amigos to look me in the eye. From initial review to final deliberations on my dismissal recommendation, we spent less than thirty minutes together. And that included me watching them shift their weight from one leg to the other in long, awkward silences at the beginning and end of our meeting.

If this was how the boys were going to respond to me, I should go through debilitating personal circumstances more often.

CHAPTER FIFTEEN

Monday, December 14

I had just enough time after my meeting with the 'village people' to call Donna and catch her up. In a previous life, she'd been a kick-butt personal injury attorney, and she hadn't lost her killer instincts. I listened to her spout off legalese long enough to write down names from her own short list of divorce attorneys. She suggested I call one before the sun set. Today.

Then she dropped a bomb by suggesting I go see a counselor—right after I told her about the strange visions and dark feelings I was experiencing. And she had an idea of who she thought I should see. So much for attorney-client privilege. Might as well tell my doctor I ate ice cream for breakfast. Just as I hung up, Mitch's customary two quick raps on the door announced her arrival right before she let herself into my office.

"How was your chat with Donna?"

I caught Mitch up on everything, including the recommendation to see a shrink.

"She give you anybody good to see?"

"Yeah," I snorted. "Kira."

"Kira?"

"Figures it'll look good for the court case she's sure will come out of this gunfight. Wants me to get right on it—made an appointment for me and everything."

"You have an appointment with Kira?"

"Yeah."

"You're going to see the she-devil shrink without being ordered to?"

"Yes. No. Well, turns out Kira'd received a friendly, off-the-record call from the sheriff, strongly suggesting she talk me into it. So much for needing to see Frank today. Took care of that with a quick call too. He wanted to ease me into the idea of seeing someone. A certain someone."

"Was that before or after he called Donna and told her what to tell you?"

"My point exactly."

"Well, happy holidays."

"Ho, ho, ho."

"When you going to see Kira?"

"Nine o'clock tomorrow morning. Why not? Might as well get it over with. I can tell by looking at you that this isn't exactly a coffee break. What's up?"

"I've got some good news and some bad news."

"Hit me. Bad news first, please."

"Well, the bad news is, you might want to reconsider the holiday party this evening."

"What? Why?"

"It's gonna be a bunch of cops who are on Del's side. He got to them before you did." Her eyes held pain and a hint of embarrassment.

I was missing something. "Mitch?"

"Del just sent in his RSVP. With a plus one on it. And a smiley face." She spit out all this information, staccato, both eyes riveted to the floor.

"What! Who does that ...? It's not enough that he's ruining me at every turn. Now he wants to embarrass me in front of the guys? He needs to be taken out!" I tried to conjure up my tough-girl act, but it fell flat and unconvincing, even to me. Especially to me.

The raw pain hung heavy between us, drowning out words and sounds and heartbeats. Every cell of my being weighed a ton. "So what's the good news?"

"Turns out there isn't any."

"Yeah. I figured. Mitch?"

"Yeah?"

"I can't go tonight," I whispered.

"I know. I'm on it."

"Thanks." I turned to face the library area in the back of my office. Shame burned across my face. I didn't want to look into the eyes of pity from a colleague—friend or foe.

"Chief?"

"Yeah?"

"You don't deserve this. I can't believe what that rat is doing, and we will not let him get away with it. We will find a way to see he gets his."

"I know." My voice was in danger of breaking, but I wasn't about to cry in front of her again today. "Thanks. I couldn't get through this without you. It gives me a world of comfort to know you'll be there in my place tonight. Now go and raise some Cain for me, would you please?"

She straightened up to go. Almost as an afterthought, she dropped a bomb of her own. "Oh, and I've taken the liberty to schedule a little meeting for you before you leave today. With Bruce."

Bruce Schofield was one of two part-time village attorneys.

"Bruce? What is it with you guys taking it upon yourselves to set up all these unwanted meetings?"

"Think about it."

"All right, not a bad political call. I get it. Look at me. I'm thrilled. What time?"

"About ten minutes ago. He's sitting outside in the reception area. I haven't mentioned a thing to him, but I don't know whether or not he's heard anything from the rumor mill. All I told him is you have a personal matter you might wish to discuss with him in private. He made himself instantly available."

"He knows."

"Yeah, that's what I figured too. Don't shoot the messenger." Mitch winked at me before turning and letting herself out.

I stepped into the reception area to greet him, and we walked into my office together.

Bruce'd come up through some unusual ranks. Harvard-educated and from a family of tremendous wealth, he'd eschewed it all and gone into the public defender's office for the bulk of his career. We all thought he had political aspirations a mile long, but turns out he just wanted to do his own version of the right thing. We shared a deep and genuine respect for each another.

"Chief Oliver, I'm sorry for your loss. I've only heard a few of the rumors, but I know enough to be extremely sorry. And to let you know if there is any way at all I may be of service or support to you in the upcoming days and weeks, I really want to be."

"Thank you. Have a seat." I turned my head to the side and looked at his reflection in the office windows. He was tall and muscular, neither fat nor slight, and always seemed to be one of those ready-for-action guys. He sure looked military to me, but he'd denied it so often that I kept my thoughts to myself. He was ruggedly handsome and wore well-cut suits. Nothing about him seemed to fit the lowly-public-servant profile he projected. But then, maybe I puzzled others, too. "Any friendly advice, one village official to another?"

"You need a lawyer. Immediately. And just a little truth—you'll be better off without him in your life. That man wasn't worthy of you. Period. He was an anchor tied to your leg—a fool, and an embarrassment to men everywhere, and he didn't deserve you. Everyone is on your side here. Everyone."

"Does it really have to come down to sides? Can't my personal life stay personal? Is there something you're trying to tell me?"

"Your personal life can't stay personal. It's way too late for that."

"What's that supposed to mean?"

"Just that I'm on your side."

"Is there something else you'd like to share with me?"

He looked at me in silence for several seconds and then shook his head. I couldn't read his eyes, but he was hiding something. Something big.

"No. Just that I'm here for you. Anytime. Please remember that."

Something in his voice gave me the chills, and my throat dried up. I stood, offered him my hand, thanked him for coming, and walked him to the door. After his exit, I sat behind my desk in the waning light. What just happened?

There was something very unsettling about Bruce's message. I wanted to believe him when he said he was on my side. And I did believe him ... until he repeated the same thing. Twice.

CHAPTER SIXTEEN

Monday, December 14

If I stayed in the station, I'd be risking more face-to-face. But who in their right mind would feel like heading to my newly barren tomb of a home no matter what Donna managed to do to it today? I stood in front of my desk and stared into nothing for way too long before I sat down and flipped open my computer. While waiting for the screen to turn from black to green to action, I fumbled around in my top left drawer and found a half-empty bag of barbeque corn nuts next to a pile of unopened mail. I pulled the mail out and plopped it on the desk.

The first envelope was a perfect square, adorned with the signature calligraphy of one of my dearest friends—Georgi. I was by her side the night she fell in love with her husband, Cliff, over stale beer and bad dancing. If only I could escape to the comfort of their cozy living room. Soon. I nudged the bag of corn nuts open, leaving it in the drawer to minimize crumbs, and popped a few tangy-sweet nuggets into my mouth. The rest of the mail was holiday cards and junk.

I sat back in my leather swivel chair as I poked at my phone screen until I reached the current files on the Mentor Sister Serial Killer. Nothing new had come in.

What mysterious force drove this psychopath toward each of his victims? What happened in his early life to drive him to such heinous acts of cruelty? Would his secret past lead us to him in time to stop another murder? And why did victimology seem to clearly indicate some sort of connection to me? I couldn't muster one shred of compassion for this killer. He needed to be captured or killed as soon as possible.

I looked at my watch. I had just enough time to stop by and see Samantha during her after-school program, but I'd have to hurry. I raced to the parking lot, pausing only to pull out my phone. Laughing, I texted the word 'incoming,' our secret code. This unexpected visit would make her so happy. I made it there in record time.

Saint Camille Catholic School spanned a city block, though that included the church, playgrounds, parking lots, and a century-old convent. I pulled my squad car to the front of the building, mindful to leave the spot marked 'Fr. Hank' vacant. I'd learned the hard way not to mess with him or his parking spot.

The hallways were dimly lit as I walked toward the cafeteria. Student art filled the walls, leaving them awash in the smell of fresh paints mixed with crayons and slow-drying paste. Both wooden doors stood open, letting loose a cacophony of happy sounds. I entered and came to a stop, scanning the room for her. Rectangular tables, seating twelve kids each, had been painstakingly set in place five deep on each side of the room.

Samantha was seated all the way at the back of the room, at the last table on the left, as far away from the door as possible. Protecting herself by losing herself in the crowd? Where was the undercover agent that Nick had set up to watch over Samantha? Sister Angela was on duty, and she noticed me before Sam did. She was standing next to a statue of Saint Theresa, facing the kids. She wore a full habit, complete with the requisite large, blocky, olivewood rosary.

"Hey, Chief! Great to see you. Are you here to take a snack break with Samantha?" Angela's voice was sweet like cotton candy, and she flooded the large space with her smile. Sam loved her, and for that reason alone, I'd do just about anything she asked of me.

"I am. I hope I'm not intruding. How much time do we have left? Would you mind if we spent a few minutes together? I probably should have called first. I'm sorry." I was falling all over myself, weak-kneed at the thought of seeing Sam. This version of "Mother May I" usually bought me an extra minute or two.

"As soon as she's done, I'm sure she'd love to show you her art project from this afternoon." Sister Angela beamed.

"I'd love to see it. On the way in, I enjoyed the lovely pieces you've already posted in the hallway. Quite a bit of talent resting here before us, I'd say."

"You could certainly say so now, though you might not have said that had you been in the room with us while we made the sausage, so to speak. Elementary art is not for the faint of heart." Her smile never faltered.

I laughed and waved at Samantha when her little head popped up with a gigantic smile as her gaze connected with mine. It took all I had not to run to her and scoop her up, but it was important to let her approach me first. She needed to make all the choices. It was one more step toward helping her heal from all of the other choices that had been torn away from her. I snuck a peek at my phone, then jammed the phone back into my pocket. *Slow your roll, Oliver.* I took an unhurried breath and watched her go about her clean-up chores. She packed her empty after-school snack items back onto her tray, only to unpack them, making sure everything was put in the right spot on the right conveyer belt at the tray return—an agonizingly slow routine.

She finished her duties and then walked in measured steps through the cafeteria. For one bright moment, she clearly wanted to run to me, but Sister Angela raised an eyebrow in Sam's direction, and she pulled herself back into a fast walk. She arrived with twinkling eyes. Then she held her right hand out, and I stepped in and took it gently. I waited for Sister Angela's nod before walking her out into the hallway.

Several steps beyond the door, Samantha's little body quivered, and she squealed happily, stepping in front of me to grab my other hand. "Miss Jo! I love you so much! I'm so glad you came to see me today!"

I knelt down and scooped her up into the gentlest of hugs. My injured shoulder didn't even hurt that much. "Oh, my darling Sam. I love you too, sweetie. Now tell me about your day at school."

I sat back on my heels and smiled as her happy little voice sang out a hundred tiny details of her day. Waves of brilliant blue water flooded my heart with impossibly beautiful feelings. All was right, and all was lovely to me, from the tiniest cell of her perfect body to the mismatched tile floor. Being with her seemed the most natural, the best, and the most important part of my life.

"I made a cow today in art class. You wanna see her?" Sam's voice was thick with admiration. She loved her cows and, by extension, so did I.

"Of course I do, baby doll. Take me to your moo-dur!" I waited for her laughter to chime in, but she looked at me, puzzled. "Get it, moo-dur? Like a cow? And a mother? Only moo-dur?"

The light clicked on, eliciting only a roll of her eyes before she grabbed me by the hand and turned to lead me down the hall to her cow. I guess it wasn't that funny.

At the end of the hall, late-afternoon winter light streamed in through the stairwell windows. She proudly pointed me to a cacophony of color on a generous piece of salmon-colored paper on the wall. It was hard to tell where the grass ended and the cow began. Or where the sky began and the cow ended. It was colorful. It was beautiful. It was Sam.

"I love this, sweetie! You're such a good artist. I have the perfect place for this in my office."

I stroked Samantha's baby-fine hair as we admired her work together. She beamed and pressed her body against my left side, leaning into me. I kept my hand on her head and breathed in deeply. If God existed like Samantha believed, maybe He could keep her safe and give her this sense of safety and peace as long and as often as possible.

Purposeful heels clacked their way toward us. I straightened up, dropping my hand to Sam's back and turned us both around. She held my hand again, and we walked back down the hallway to the line of her classmates. We let go of each other's hands, and I bent down to kiss her. She hugged me quickly and then turned and skipped before remembering to walk the last few feet to be the last in line. She nodded up at Sister Angela, and then turned to smile and wave at me. I watched until she rounded the corner of the staircase, heading toward the after-school activities room on the second floor.

The waning light outside reminded me I was done for the day. But there was one more person my heart yearned to see.

Thirty minutes later, I stood in a crowded Mexican restaurant teeming with life on the city's north side, scanning the room for my swarthy friend, Gino Rivera. There—a colorful interruption in the dark sea of dress uniforms and business suits. Gino had taken up residence in a back corner booth.

When he stood to wave me over, his holstered gun was apparent on his right hip, nicely balanced by the large trucker's wallet in his back left pocket, silver chain linking it neatly to a belt loop in the front. He stood there, waiting for me, his broad grin displaying perfect, white teeth, and I couldn't help but laugh out loud as I made my way over to him.

"Mama mia! You look good enough to eat, *m'hija*. I should look half so good as you do." Gino wrapped me up in his huge, bear arms, his tasteful citrus scent enveloping me.

"It's so good to see you. I needed a Gino hug." I pulled back from him, straightening my uniform jacket and repositioning my purse.

Gino was a man of many talents. People often underestimated him because they couldn't look past his do-rag and trucker's wallet. Inside his shaggy, affable, Cuban head was a mastermind at work. He was always inventing new criminal restraints, honing his private, patented collection of "catch-and-release accessories," as he referred to them. He split his genius into equal parts by devoting a ton of time and energy to making big money by marketing his wares. He was adept at both ends of the business. He was also very good at reading my mind and calming my emotions.

"Now, sit. Tell me everything. Especially all that I can do for the woman with the biggest heart in the universe."

His warm voice and caring heart were just what the doctor ordered, and I relaxed with each word we exchanged. He drank cola, but I opted for a frosty draw of dark beer. After giving him the thumbnail version of my misery over the first two beers, we ordered dinner, and I slugged down two more beers. I grew maudlin and moved into murkier territory, eventually working in tomorrow's looming visit with Kira.

"M'hija, don't you think you've had enough to drink?"

"Not yet." I took another sip and wiped the foam from my mouth before asking, "What keeps a life from unraveling, Gino?"

Silent, he considered my question for what seemed like an eternity. I drained the last drop of my stout Mexican beer while I waited.

"M'hija, this life is a gift, even on the most cursed of days. Even today, when you find yourself alone, you may meet the One who is most powerful in your weakness. You will know one day what I say is true. Today is a gift, and every minute of this day has a purpose hidden in it for you. You can live each day, embracing your life."

Well, that had been worth the wait. Although, halfway into his second sentence, my head had started swimming. I vowed to switch to root beer next. "But there's nothing left for me. Everywhere I turn, I'm lost. I thought I knew how to live at work until everyone started taking sides, but I don't know how to live with a literally empty house. I've got nothing left. How do I live from the moment I get home to the moment I crawl back to work? It's like my life has turned into one long stint of solitary confinement. I can't stand the thought of living the rest of my life like this."

"But how can you think you are alone when Gino is right here next to you, plying you with free nachos? When all around you are people who love you? What about Nick? He's also your good friend, no? What is it that compels you to spend your time in darkness rather than walking with me, with God, in the light? I can see you are in a lot of pain, but I'm here to tell you there is more for you, Josephine. God has a life of power and glory and unending love waiting for you to accept from His outstretched hand."

He stopped abruptly as I rolled my eyes at him.

The beer was losing its effect on me. "Please, not tonight. I don't want to hear the God-thing tonight."

Gino had lived a lot of life, and I felt bad whining to him and then shutting him down like that, but the last thing I wanted to hear right now was a bunch of religious mumbo-jumbo.

"Come to church with me tonight, m'hija. He will prove himself to you."

"I don't think so, Gino, but thanks for asking."

His eyes saddened. I looked down at the table and scooted toward the open end of the booth's bench.

He stood up and hugged me as I prepared to leave. "Come and see me when you need a friend. I'm always here for you." Then he pulled out his cell and called me a cab. "I am such a good friend that I won't let you drive home in your condition. No arguments, please."

"Thanks, Gino. I'll call you soon." I couldn't meet his eyes before I turned and walked out into the cold to wait for my ride.

CHAPTER SEVENTEEN

Monday, December 14

I heaved myself out of the taxi and stumbled to the house. When was the last time I'd taken a cab home from dinner in the city? How much had I drunk? Who was I becoming? More importantly, where were my house keys? My head spun like a tilt-a-whirl, making it hard to rifle through my pockets and purse in the dark.

Fiddling with the key, I swore like a longshoreman and fumbled with the doorknob as I unlocked the door. It was stuck. Finally, I twisted the knob in anger. The weight of my shoulder pushing against the solid wood forced the issue. The door swung inward. A thick cloud of fury swirled about me, settling on my shoulders, weighing me down. Pinpricks of goosebumps skittered over my arms as I peered into the darkness. I grabbed the holstered pistol resting at the bottom of my bag and wrenched it free. The home-sweet-home feel of my most trusted partner comforted my strained muscles. I released the magazine to verify it was full, then partially racked the slide to view the round in the chamber.

I nearly had to pull my unresponsive feet up with my hands to get them to move me from the foyer into the empty kitchen and great room area. I reached the two-story room, breathing hard, looking over my shoulder. I took a deep breath and snapped on the light.

The room was alien to me.

Faint kick-mark dents lingered under a new coat of white paint on the walls. Donna's restoration project included a green sofa from her basement, staged in the middle of the room.

I sagged down into the folds of the old sofa, but the presence I'd sensed in the foyer had followed me. I stood up and took several testing steps in and out of the room. A palpable evil shadow stuck close to me, tracking me like some cosmic bloodhound. Or was it the alcohol? I took several deep breaths to clear my head.

I pulled out my phone. There was a text message from Mitch, stating that Del had shown up to the holiday party solo after all. So the "plus one" was still a mystery. Instead of calling Nick, Donna, or Mitch, I thumbed through my favorite pictures featuring me and the man I thought I knew. Melancholy memories flooded in, chased by longing and regret. Why did everything change after Del and I got married? Why had I put up with his abuse for so many years? I wanted someone to love and cherish me. But it wasn't Del. It had never been Del. That was clear now.

The raging presence beside me seemed to soften as my sorrow grew, inviting me to lean into it, to find my comfort in its muddy shadow. I returned to the sofa, and the darkness wrapped around me like a shroud.

I wept.

Del had chosen someone else. I clenched my jaw. Animal sounds growled in my throat. Would he be happier without me? Worse yet, happier with someone else? How long had he been cheating on me? My eyes latched onto the honeymoon picture in my phone's gallery—the handsome, dimpled face of the man I thought I'd loved. He'd left haunting memories and a thousand broken promises in his wake. The crushing existence of his mistress mocked me.

The dark presence pulled at me. I still held the pistol in my right hand, and I pointed it up, admiring its sleek lines. The gun was one of the few standbys I could still call my own, and

I respected the solid bond between us. At least the cold steel had not abandoned me.

The shadow offered me glimpses of my lonely, new world—disturbing images of myself embittered, friendless and alone. It offered me two choices—succumb to the darkness and live in subjection to an obscenely evil presence, or continue to resist it. The notion of resistance felt like being battered by gale-force winds while carrying an impossibly heavy load down a rickety dock toward an ocean-liner-shaped mirage. Heading out to unknown seas.

A craving bubbled up from deep within me—steely and insistent. If this was my new life, I didn't want it. I wouldn't choose it. Not for another fifty years. Not for another fifty minutes. Death beckoned like a soft bed, and I sat there, silent and still. What would I do next?

A blissful release and quiet pleasure would be mine if only I allowed my gun's barrel to nestle against the roof of my mouth. The dark being wrapped itself around me. I welcomed its burn.

I slipped the safety off and peered into the chamber of the pistol, relishing the sound and smell of it. The silvery-copper bullet lay there, eager and open-hearted, waiting for my command. I raised the stout barrel and rested it on my chin, squeezing my eyes shut. Was there a glimmer of hope anywhere within? One good reason to live, just one, and I'd be okay for another day. The dark presence growled around me, urging me to pull the trigger.

Samantha's sunlit figure appeared. She was holding Nick's hand and Gino's hand. All of them glowed with a nuclear joy as warmth flooded my heart. Stone shields slammed down like a theatre curtain. Samantha was replaced with tawdry visions of Del and his new woman, drowning out hope, extinguishing any remaining sparks of joy. Demonic shadows clung to both figures. My gut sloshed. Goosebumps ran up and down my arms. The rank odor of rotten eggs assaulted my nose, mouth, and lungs.

You're not wanted here. You'd be better off dead. You hate it here. You're miserable. Come to me, and I will give you rest. Just one little sting is all you'll feel. Come on, let's get this over with.

My breathing stopped as I obediently opened my mouth just wide enough to welcome the pistol home. The metallic promise of the barrel rose to my lips, but I paused just before going all the way. The grotesqueries swirled on. I put my left hand over my eyes and shut them tight, gun poised and ready in my right.

A shimmering image broke through the black haze. A majestic white horse thundered toward me—galloping, throwing its handsome head up into the clear-blue sky behind him. He whinnied at me.

Hope emerged, eclipsing my pain.

I leaned into the vision as the powerful animal pounded closer. He extended his long, beautiful neck to me in greeting, nostrils flaring. I could almost feel his warm, sweet breath caressing my face.

What am I doing? I withdrew the barrel and released the magazine into my hand in one proficient motion. I pushed myself away from the dark presence and rose to my feet. The brilliance of the moonlight through the kitchen window melted away my anxiety.

I secured my weapon in the gun safe embedded in the wall near the chimney. With an urge to go riding, I marched to the hall closet for my hunt boots and riding pants, then folded them by the front door. Maybe I'd have time to hit the barn tomorrow after my stint with Kira the shrink.

I should've gone to church with Gino tonight. Two powerful forces warred within me, shoving aside anything I knew about grace and victory. Yes, I should've gone to church tonight.

CHAPTER EIGHTEEN

Tuesday, December 15

"You have such beautiful skin." Heat rolled up my sternum to my throat. A taxi ride and five long minutes of small talk with Kira the Shrink had brought me to that pathetic statement. Did it sound as weird to her as it did in my head?

The two large mugs of coffee I'd poured down my gullet earlier this morning to compensate for my beer fest last night weren't helping. Tension snaked its way up my neck and dug into my forehead. Both temples pounded, and nausea churned in the pit of my stomach. My forehead felt like a lighthouse, blaring through the night, drumming out my secret over and over: Del left me! Del left me! Del left me for another woman!

I sat stone-still on Kira's sleek, leather couch. Could she see the truth shining through the surface of my anger? I hated small talk.

"Thank you. If only it were half as beautiful as yours, I wouldn't think of bothering with these silly creams and such." Her faux, warm laughter was followed by the slightest shrug of her shoulders and a perfectly timed, breathless sigh. "Alas, I treat myself to only the finest moisturizers, and that, twice a day. Who're we kidding? Just between us girls—three times a day, most days. But don't tell my therapist."

She leaned forward and issued a conspiratorial wink. Her aura seemed off today. Most days I didn't like the vibe, and I didn't like her. But hey, I had issues, so I let it slide. It was probably yet another manifestation of my well-developed denial system working overtime. She seemed odder than usual today, though, even for her. I probably couldn't blame it on my hangover. She kept turning a small round jar in her right hand, as if the green glass housed a mysterious power.

She lightly tossed it from hand to hand and turned her attention from the jar to me. Was she angry? Glad to see me? I couldn't tell. "I'd offer you some, but it would be completely wasted on you and an insult to boot. Your beauty is equaled only by your valor. Now, which is it that brings you here today?"

She switched back and forth from super-annoying-borderline-psycho in my book, to best friend, to grandmotherly therapist at lightning speed. Trying to catch me off guard? Trigger some response? Who knew?

I wasn't even sure why I was there myself. Maybe that was the point. "Yeah, well, you got a call, didn't you?"

She smiled, crossed her legs, reached for her computer tablet, and sat back in her chair, all in one smooth motion. Her skirt rode up well past her knees, and I compared my own shaky demeanor to her polished confidence. I was definitely going to reward myself with some very fine chocolate once this visit was over. Maybe some red wine to go with it.

"Jo, Jo, Jo, what are we going to do with you? Your humility amuses and impresses. But come now, we must have some feelings to discuss together today, do we not?"

This was going from uncomfortable to weird. She was teasing me. I just wanted to be done—to get back to my office, and get back to the serial killer case.

"Well, first off, I hate him."

"Mmm, go on." Her smile had grown Cheshire-like.

"Aren't you going to write this down?"

"Now, Jo, you know I never forget a thing you say. Do go on."

"What can I say? You know the story. I really don't want to tell it again. I did my job. I was a pretty good wife. Del cheated—found somebody else. And I'd be lying to say I don't hate him. Shoot, I hate myself. And I'm so angry, I could kill him with my bare hands."

"What about his friend? Do you want to kill her with your bare hands too? Why don't we start there?" She smiled, clearly enjoying this. She was evil.

A wave of darkness came over me, jumbling my thoughts. The pounding in my temples worsened, and I got so dizzy I thought I might fall over. Horrible pictures from my marriage and from the Mentor Sister Serial Killer crime scenes merged. I tried to edge away from the terrible bits and pieces of pictures floating around me, but I could barely move—like I was trying to walk through a force field of cosmic molasses.

As the dark consumed me, bone-deep, razor-sharp fear gripped me, but at the moment the unseen darkness overpowered me, a light space opened up in the far reaches of my mind. A deep peace spread through me, relaxing my body, freeing my mind and calming my spirit.

Strong, clear words bubbled up from nowhere. "I know my sheep, and my sheep know me." I stared at the movie screen in my mind's eye as another set of crystal-clear words took shape. "You, dear children, are from God and have overcome them, because the one who is in you is greater than the one who is in the world."

The dark pictures faded away, replaced by a sweet-smelling field of prairie flowers in a sunny valley, housed between lush mountains, on a beautiful day. A Magnificent Being stepped out from behind one of the mountains and revealed Himself to me. Somehow I knew He was God. He was glorious and beautiful beyond description. In His arms, He tenderly carried a little girl. He held her as if she were His only child.

It was me in His arms—a little girl version of me.

He wrapped His strong arms around my little-girl self, overwhelming me with feelings of warmth and safety, peace and power. I closed my eyes for a moment, leaning into His pure warmth. A strength I didn't know I had grew from deep within me. I smiled and opened my eyes.

Whatever had just gone on in my head, I didn't understand. My strength returned. My deepest sense of self—my balance, hope, and peace—was restored. The presence and the power of God sat next to me on the sofa. His Spirit was so real, I could almost touch Him. His light warmed me, rocking me to the depths of my soul.

In the vision, where once there had been darkness and pain, now there was peace. And through the warmth came the same message again. "Greater is the one who is in you than the one who is in the world."

I didn't know where those words came from, or how long that vision had played out in my head. Was it a moment? An hour? A day? Had Kira seen it too? The vision had shown me how my life could look, if I would acknowledge God existed and invite Him into a relationship with me. God would live inside me and He would conquer the darkness on my behalf.

My confusion disappeared. I knew why I was there and how I would answer her questions about my mental health so that I could get clearance to return to work. I kept my head down in a show of false humility, allowing her to continue to assert authority over me. She'd been silent during my inner turmoil. What was she thinking?

It was time to put an exit plan in motion. "Kira, my marriage was bad. Del was and is an abusive jerk. I didn't deserve what he did to me. I can't change what happened, but I'll survive this." I took a deep breath to calm myself. "And Del? I haven't even begun to think about him. I'm devastated. I'm overwhelmed. But I'll get through this. I'm not alone. End of story. Now, why don't you sign this release, and let's call it a day."

God nudged me, and I opened my purse, grabbed the fitness-for-duty form, and handed it to her.

She had me over a barrel, and she knew it. I could return to duty without being formally evaluated, but she knew I wanted to be a role model to my staff. How many times had I forced my staff to her office as an unofficial way of clearing them before returning to work? *Time to put your money where your mouth is, Oliver.* I braced myself for her next assault. I fully expected a fight, more of the twisted repartee she'd started this session with. Instead, there was more silence.

She sat back in her chair, eyes narrowed. She held her fancy pen between slender fingers. She never once looked at the page as she signed, dated, and returned it.

I rose to my feet. God's warmth, His comfort, and His presence enveloped me. I couldn't wait to tell Gino about my encounter with what had to be the one true God. I turned, giving Kira an over-the-shoulder glance, as I walked out her door without another word.

CHAPTER NINETEEN

Tuesday, December 15

I left Kira's office with peace, trimmed in what could only be described as joy. Not that happy Christmas morning kind of joy, but something more profound and far-reaching. The lingering sweetness of the moment I'd experienced with that Magnificent Being in the meadow filled me with longing to return to His presence. Every part of my life seemed to be shifting and changing at such a rapid rate, even this new bundle of oppositional forces didn't surprise me. Who knew what would happen next? I just hoped He would be there to help me face whatever came next—whenever.

When the taxi dropped me off, the police station was a ghost town. I arranged for my squad car to be retrieved from the Mexican restaurant. After that, it was easy to dodge any meaningful human contact and hide out in my office until mid-afternoon, sorting holiday cards, reading reports, and surfing the federal databases in search of clues about the Mentor Sister Serial Killer. Mitch could handle this evening's ceremony at the college just fine without me. I was clicking open another file when my desk phone rang.

"Chief Oliver."

"Hey, Josie."

"Nick! Just the man I'm looking for."

"Well, I'm glad to hear that … finally."

"Calm down, tiger. I was just searching through ViCAP for updates. You got anything?"

"No. He's remained dormant so far."

"Good. I hope we make it through the holidays this quiet. I've got enough horrors of my own."

"One woman's horror is another man's opportunity. When you coming home? You must've opened all your holiday greetings and moved your pens from one corner of your desk to another enough by now."

"Home? What do you mean by 'home' exactly?"

"Why don't you come on home and find out? I've decided to stick close to you for the foreseeable future. And you seem to have plenty of room right now, so I didn't think you'd mind if I rented out a spot in your basement."

"As in the one located underneath my house?"

He laughed. "Yes."

"Without even asking me or checking to make sure I have a renter's permit?"

"I bought groceries."

"Coffee?"

"Of course."

"Ice cream?"

"C'mon, beautiful. You won't even know I'm here. I'll be the model boarder. Besides, with the way this case is going, you'll see my pretty face only at the station. See you in twenty."

He hung up before I could object, and I sat alone for a moment, smiling. I wouldn't have to face my empty life completely alone. I'd never really been a landlord before, but how hard could it be?

CHAPTER TWENTY

Tuesday, December 15

"Hi, honey. I'm home!" I couldn't resist tossing the comfortable refrain to Nick as I walked through the door. Delicious Italian aromas lured me down the hall into the kitchen, and I wondered out loud if he might like to resign his current position and cook for me full time. I assured him his sauces alone would make it worth the expense.

He tossed me an apron from across the kitchen. "Baby, it'll take more than your sauce-whipped self flattering me to even make me consider working for you. But your love for all things Nick does give you an edge over the current competition. And being the mercenary I am, I'm perfectly willing to give you the opportunity to court me."

I stepped around the island as he finished his retort and hugged him hard enough to stop his talking for half a breath. The telltale key lay on the counter. Another mystery solved. Must've gotten it from Donna. He kissed me on the forehead, gently pulling away as he looked me up and down and resumed his speech.

"But not in that outfit. Why don't you head upstairs and throw on some jeans while I finish up this sauce? I've got something I want to run by you when you come down."

"Okay."

I stood in the archway, watching him for a moment, overwhelmed with peace and joy. My short solitary confinement had opened to let in a little light, offering me enough clarity to see that I was never alone. Even in those darkest moments, I'd been surrounded by the love of a God who sought me, even though I hated Him, hated myself. My heart swelled with gratitude. Gratitude? Me? Where'd that come from? I liked this new feeling. A lot.

Halfway up the stairs, I paused. Something was different. The stairwell had been repainted! And not only painted, but plastered. Each and every garish hole kicked or scratched into these walls not three days ago had been smoothed over and painted, erasing all evidence of my angry, exiting, soon-to-be-ex-husband.

At the top of the stairs, the woodwork glimmered all glossy and bright. Donna and her merry band of carpenters even managed to touch up the baseboards all the way up the stairs and around this little landing. The door to my bedroom looked brand new. As I entered the room, I stopped to take it all in, hugging myself.

The last time I stood there, the walls were ugly, bare, and broken—windows left open, curtains and shades ripped down, wall mountings half in and half out. Nick and Donna had completely cleaned up the room. They must've hired carpet and window cleaners too. They'd had the walls and ceiling painted bright white, and one long, windowless wall featured yellow wallpaper adorned with white roses, capped by a simple white wooden chair rail running from corner-to-corner. I'd walked into a new beginning.

Underneath a panel of windows that overlooked the small lake near my home sat a folded pair of worn and faded blue jeans. Donna had chosen my all-time favorite brand of jeans in my size and laid them out on the freshly cleaned carpet underneath this sunny spot. She'd even washed them. An old FBI hoodie was sprawled out over a walnut chair in the corner of the windowed alcove. I kicked off my navy pumps, dropped my skirt to the floor and ditched my nylons. My feet sank into the plush carpet. I grabbed the sun-warmed jeans off the floor.

The soft, worn fabric caressed my thighs as I tugged the jeans into place by the belt loops and fastened the button fly.

I took off my suit jacket and teased my silk blouse over my head, squirming happily into the fleece hoodie before hurrying back down to the kitchen.

Nick turned and flashed a hundred-watt smile. "You look great." He handed me a cup of strong, fresh coffee. "You're gonna live, sweetheart. I know it may not feel like it, but you're gonna live. Now drink up. I added cream and sweetener… just the way you like it."

"Nick, I …"

"Just relax. I'm here for you, and I'm going to do everything in my power to bring you out of this black hole and keep you safe."

"You shouldn't … you didn't have to …"

I was a blubbering idiot. Words failed me as I struggled to share my deepest gratitude with my best friend. Without success. All I could do was stand in front of him, with my heart in my hands. He caressed my cheek and moved a strand of hair away from my face.

"It's what friends do for each other. It's nothing but a coat of paint, a couple of ounces of putty, and a few favors called in from some guys who owe me. There's much more to come over the next couple of weeks. Christmas came early. And nothing's free, babe. You know that. I already have a few ideas for a little quid pro quo when you feel up to tackling our serial killer case again. Plus, you haven't made me coffee in years." He laughed, and mischief twinkled in his eyes.

"Yeah, right. Like you'd even let me make you coffee. You're impossible to please. I'd have to buy an espresso machine and make you one of those fancy drinks. And I'd never get the temperature and the foam just right."

"Oh, don't worry. I have much bigger plans for you than that, my friend."

"Do tell. And please make sure said plans involve some shopping on the side."

"Snap out of it. I got business on the brain. I got a special little project, and I think you can help me out like no one else can."

"What?"

"Ah …" He stepped closer. "You're just going to have to join me for dinner if you want to hear what I have in mind for you. And, by the way, you look amazing in those jeans. Love your bare feet."

Nick launched into an opera song and pulled a smile out of me as I padded over to the counter. I drained my coffee and set the cup in the sink. He turned and offered me a delicately stemmed crystal glass of sparkling water.

"These aren't my glasses."

"Housewarming gift … from me."

"Thanks. You have great taste in crystal." I smiled and took a sip.

"So, Nomad's coming up for pre-trial."

"Nomad?"

"Sure. Nomad. You gotta get out more. Read a paper, watch the news. Take your mind off your own worries."

I stared at him.

He rolled his eyes as if talking to a fourth grader and continued. "Okay, let's review. Two days ago, a guy who calls himself Nomad—real name's Cal Terry—became instantly famous during an evening homeowners' association meeting north of here. Ringing any bells?"

"Okay, yeah, but not all the details." A sick feeling gurgled in my stomach. I remembered it all right. I just didn't want to.

"Nomad is the all-American dad who decided to reduce living expenses by whacking his entire family. Left 'em in the basement while he tried to figure out what to do with them. Long enough to get a fine from his HOA for foul odors. Ticked him off, so he decided to go to the next board meeting of the association … armed."

"Right, I do remember. Turned out there was an off-duty cop on the board, who noticed something strange about Nomad from the get-go, and just happened to have his own piece on the ready, right?" I drank the cool, lemony water while Nick placed white dinner plates on the counter. I had forgotten the guy's name. "I just thought of him as Crazy Homeowner Guy." I added forks and knives to the place settings.

"Makes sense, given the media blitz. That's exactly how he was referred to at the time." Nick turned to inspect the pasta boiling on the stove.

"Didn't homeowner Terry go off somewhere during the meeting, and the cop jumped him?" I turned to open the fridge, searching for a refill.

"Yeah, but it was right up front, during the public comments portion of the meeting. And the off-duty cop was a woman. She gave him the eye, and he freaked, but she had her weapon out before he could take the safety off his .38."

I poured myself another glass of the soothing liquid. "And that was when everybody panicked and fled."

"Yep. One guy even jumped out a window, which was pathetic as it was right next to the door, and his wife, who he completely forgot all about, was left standing alone in the line of fire." He headed toward the sink, colander in hand.

"Oh, yeah. Then in the confusion, the off-duty cop shot the perp in the leg and cuffed him before he knew what hit him. What a piece of work that guy was. And what a shame about the psycho's family." I shook my head, trying not to picture the crime scene.

"That's Nomad. Given that he was carrying a concealed weapon, they got a search warrant for other firearms, and that's when they found his family members in an advanced stage of decomp in the basement."

"Each one with a clean hole in the head. Twenty-two caliber, execution style. Some family man. Why the sudden interest in Terry?" I dug out some paper napkins from a bag on the counter.

"Well, the crime happened just about on the state line, and jurisdiction's been a battle. His house was in Paradise County, which is where the bodies were found, but the HOA's clubhouse is located in Wisconsin, which is where the takedown happened. So, Nomad's got a court date coming up next week here in Paradise County, and he needs an escort from the jail in Springfield to the local courthouse. That's where you come in."

"Why me? I've got no interest or jurisdiction in this case. Besides, the FBI took over, and the evidence couldn't be clearer. So what's the deal? He into something bigger? What's in this for you? Or me, for that matter?"

"This is still speculation, but a guy like him, he'd be a pretty good match for our unsub. He traveled a lot on his job. We can't prove it yet, but he looks real good for the Mentor Sister Serial Killer. And it coincides with the silence on his end. Lotta times these guys escalate for the holidays. It's a longshot, I know. Anyway, I wanted you to do the babysitting of him during his transport to the court hearing."

The holidays? I hadn't made the connection between our killer and the holiday season. Until now. A cream-colored envelope. An uneven, black scrawl. My first, middle, and last name—handwritten. A Christmas seal on the back. The blood drained from my face, and a dull pounding started in my temples.

Nick stopped his meal prep and studied my face. "What is it?"

"I got an odd Christmas card at the station a few weeks back. I didn't think anything of it. I honestly just thought it was from some well-meaning village official and put it up with the rest of my cards. It's probably nothing."

"What's probably nothing?"

"Well, didn't the Mentor Sister Serial Killer send personal notes to his victims before making contact with them? And find a benign way to meet them before making the grab?"

"Yes." His eyes narrowed, and his body tensed as he leaned toward me.

"This may not be connected, but the more I think about it, the more it's giving me the chills. The note wasn't signed—not really."

"Was it signed with a letter, or an initial?"

"It didn't look like anything at the time. It just looked like, you know, a smudge or something. Never mind. Let's just drop it."

"Humor me, Josie. What did the note say?" He leaned back on the counter, arms folded.

"Something to the tune of 'Merry Christmas, Chief. Enjoy the holiday season.'"

"That's not ringing any alarm bells for me."

"That's not all. On the back of the card, he wrote a little New Year's inscription." The pounding in my temples was no longer dull. I grabbed my purse off the counter and rummaged around until I found a bottle of aspirin. I poured three into my hand. "Give me a refill, would you, please?"

We both watched the clear liquid as he poured it from the sleek water bottle. He put the bottle down, handed my glass back to me, and looked at me so hard I turned my eyes away from his.

"What did it say?"

I gulped down the aspirin. "All the best in the New Year. Live each day like it might be your last."

"Where is it?"

"In my office." My breath came fast and shallow. I grabbed the counter edge to steady myself.

"That didn't strike you as odd until now?"

"No, I honestly kind of liked it. I thought it was from a country-western song when I read it. I didn't take it as a threat."

Nick's eyes were angry slits. His voice had taken on a dangerous tone. "Yeah. None of his vics did."

CHAPTER TWENTY-ONE

Tuesday, December 15

My Christmas card admission cast a somber note over our evening. In spite of the delicious food and all I had to be grateful for, I couldn't keep myself from veering down the Nomad brick road. Nick was no better. He showed me the mug shots of Mr. Terry, but I didn't recognize him. So that part didn't seem to match the Mentor Sister case. After dispatching a team of agents to my office to enter the card into evidence, Nick was pacing my living room.

My nerves jumped into overdrive. "So, what now? What are you doing about this guy?"

"Take it easy. He's behind bars, remember? No threat there. My biggest worry with this case is on the evidence front. I spent an hour questioning him myself the other day, and I'm telling you, I think he's good for it. I can feel it, but we can't prove it. Yet. We will though."

"Well, now, I'm suddenly interested in your babysitting commission. It'll give me pleasure to get this sick psycho to the church on time."

"Oh, no. That deal's off."

"It most certainly is not!" My voice rose an octave or two. "Now I care about this—a lot—and Gino will too. I guarantee you that."

"We want to keep this one under wraps—ship and flip him over the holidays, fly under the media radar in case anyone connects the dots. I figured you could use the distraction of guarding the transport bus. But we need to rethink that now."

His tone was crisp. I frowned. "What, now that the guy could be a real threat, you want a real cop on escort duty? Nice, Nick. Real nice."

"You know that's not what I meant."

"It's not like we'll be driving the bus. He'll be in cuffs and have like four armed guards on him in an armored vehicle, right?"

"Something like that."

"And, if I know you, you've probably already lined up Gino to be my driver."

"Maybe."

"Which would mean I'd be getting a trip to town on the state's dime, if I'm not mistaken."

"You don't miss a trick, do you?"

"This job's a piece of cake. Why wouldn't I jump at it?"

"Oh, I don't know. Maybe because you're human, and you're not half as tough as you'd like the world to believe. This guy could be hard core. And you could be next on his list. I can't risk that. It's too close to home. You can sit this one out." Nick's voice resonated with concern.

"I've been sitting out way too much, for way too long, and look where it's gotten me. What's the big deal? Gino and me, sitting in a van, trailing the big, bad, stupidly expensive Illinois Department of Corrections super bus. What could be safer than being with Gino in a van over a holiday weekend? And besides, it's not like I've got any big plans at the moment."

"You got me there. I'm out of objections. But I will say this, if anything pops on this case, and this guy starts looking better as our unsub, all bets are off. We'll start with sending your card to the lab. See if it starts singing."

"I can get behind that."

"All right then. Let's have some dessert and talk about something more pleasant—like your divorce."

CHAPTER TWENTY-TWO

Friday, December 18

I'd spent the next few days out of the office, tending to my wounded pride, canceling the timeshare in Maui, hanging with Jim, Donna, and Nick, and going back and forth from the gym to the local stable where I boarded my horse. By the time Friday rolled around, I was more than ready for a change of scenery.

Nick propped me up with strong coffee and visions of spending a day with Gino, and I got on the road before six a.m. to beat rush hour on my way south to Springfield. Hot coffee, talk radio, and two books on tape kept me company as I drove my chief of police squad car. After a while, the hypnotizing effect of the familiar drive took hold. Roadside markers rolled by in slow motion, relentless in the monotony of yet another trip down Highway 55. Mile after mile of flat, barren landscape napped on the side of the road, fully clothed in winter with the promise of slick roads wrapped in short, dark days.

I reviewed the events of the past week in vivid detail, frame by agonizing frame. As the jagged scenes lingered and endlessly dull scenery blurred past, my eyelids grew heavy, and I caught myself nodding off for a second. I needed to take a little break, so I hit buttons intermittently to haul the power windows up and down.

The chilly air revived me, and I caught the flash of a green-and-white road sign just in time to read the name of the sleepy little bedroom community: Dellesville. Not where I was pulling off, no matter how tired I was. Until the sign informed me it was another forty-eight miles between Dellesville and the next exit.

The exit ramp appeared on my right. I jerked the steering wheel without letting up on the gas, semi-mindful of the cars and trucks behind me, and was rewarded with angry looks and a little horn honking as I careened up the ramp.

I came to an abrupt stop at the intersection. To my right was a strip mall. A full-service gas station boasting of diesel fuel, Wisconsin brats, and showers by the hour flanked the mini-mall. I turned left instead, drawn to the red-and-white awning of a decent fast-food restaurant. I was momentarily hypnotized by the hazy dream of a large turtle sundae with salted pecans.

I eased into a spot adjacent to the handicapped parking near the restaurant door. William Green's name flashed up on my car monitor half a second before the phone rang. I answered it mid ring.

"What's up, William?" Phone manners tended to evaporate the minute Samantha's social worker called.

"Hello, Jo. Everything's fine with Samantha, so please put your mind at ease." The tension in his voice belied his command to relax.

"But?"

"But, there's something I just want to run by you." His baritone voice rose an octave.

"Go on." I straightened in my seat.

"Samantha's foster parents have noticed a woman in the neighborhood. She's not exactly menacing, but there's something off about her."

"Go on." My hand brushed my weapon. It remained at the ready, tucked away in my shoulder harness.

"Evidently, this woman has been hanging around the playground in a park up the street. At first she said she was a nanny, so no one thought twice about it … until yesterday afternoon. Four of the five sets of parents who regularly see each other at the playground met at the same coffee shop and started comparing stories." Paper rustled quietly, as though he was reading his notes.

"And?" My brows furrowed hard enough to form permanent wrinkles on the spot.

"And the phrase, 'I thought she was theirs,' came out of all four couples when it was reported later. Along with, 'She seemed innocent enough.'" It sounded like he was tapping his pen against the desk. William was a retired cop. His do-unto-others core couldn't retire, so he had returned to school for a degree in social work the day after he left the force. My hero.

"I still hear a 'but.' Why did the parents report her?" My spidey senses were on high alert.

"She was asking about Samantha. At least, we think she was asking about Samantha." He paused.

My heart stopped beating, and a cold stillness enveloped me. "She was asking what about Samantha? Did she use her actual name? Did she know who Sam was? How do you know it was Sam she was interested in?"

"We're not positive. She told two sets of neighbors she was a nanny for the Stevens family, one street over. She asked about the Christmas pageant. Said she loved the little donkey and thought she'd steal the show. But she also talked about the kids playing Mary and Joseph. So, it really could be any of them." His voice thinned out, and I struggled to hear him.

Samantha was playing a wise man in the pageant, so maybe this was nothing. "So why the call?"

"Doesn't matter which one she was interested in, Chief. The Stevens don't have a nanny."

"That just rang the creep-o-meter at seven bells." I gripped the steering wheel, my knuckles turning from pink to white.

"Yeah, I thought so too. Could be she's just a real pageant aficionada."

"Yeah. Could be."

"Could be just another one of your garden variety nut jobs too." William-the-cop was in full force.

"Could be."

"But, just in case, I did take the liberty of asking some old pals to run the descriptions I got of the mystery woman, but we hit nothing but brick walls and dead ends." William had been an excellent cop.

"So, for now, we don't know what we don't know. And we live with the ambiguity. And pay for some off-duty pals to watch my little girl every time she leaves the house. Definitely during all rehearsals and performances of the pageant. At the very least." Since I couldn't be there, I wanted fierce warriors with modern weapons surrounding my girl at all times. I wanted the impossible: I wanted her to stay one-hundred percent safe.

"I say we just hang tight and circle the wagons for now. Keeping an eye out is a good idea, but paying some off-duty cops to pack a little heat seems kinda—"

"Kinda like what you'd be doing if you were in my position?" Hot lava rushed through me, pushing its way up my back and into my throat.

"Maybe. Maybe it's a lot like what I'd be doing. Maybe it's overkill by two paranoid cops. I don't know. I just wanted you to know everything I know and now you do. A word of advice?"

"From you, William? Any time, any place." I opened up my palms, flexing my fingers.

"I don't like the way this sounds any more than you do. But we've done all we can, and now that I've flattened you with all the bad news, here's some great news. Samantha's currently with her foster family on a one-day skiing vacation far, far from here. And you and me and Mitch are the only ones having this conversation. So you've got some room to take a breath. Get some relief from all this stuff you've had piling up on those shoulders of yours and live a little." William had made the switch from cop back to social worker in less than ten seconds.

"All right, William, I hear you."

"Please take care of yourself in the middle of this mess. You know the score—deep breaths, good thoughts, and the occasional ice-cream sundae. Whatever it takes to stay relaxed in the midst of the storms of life, right?" The warmth behind his words calmed me down like a hug.

I looked up at the fast-food place where I'd parked and smiled. "William, I'm going to take this as a sign from God. I'm staring at a poster of ice-cream cones."

He laughed. "Well, then, go with God, Chief. I think my work is done here."

"I think so, too. Thanks, William. I'll be in touch."

A quick call to some good officers who could stand to earn some money from private security took care of my worries about Samantha when she got home from skiing. When I slid out of the squad car, my reflection in the full-length windows gave me pause. Dress blues were a social requirement for state events, and I'd worn mine for the trip down. I cut quite a striking figure as I shut the car door, even with bloodshot eyes. I unbuttoned my jacket, put my hand on my hip, admiring the way my belt nipped in my waist. A middle-aged couple beat me to the door just as I walked up the ramp, and the man held the door open for both his wife and me.

"Women and officers first," he said as he openly admired my service weapon. "Nice piece there, ma'am."

The wife jabbed an elbow into her husband's thick waist as he whistled his approval, rolling her eyes at him and offering an apology to me all at once.

I smiled without breaking my gait. "Thanks. Came with the jacket."

I stepped past them into another line and ordered an extra-large turtle sundae with a large diet cola chaser. I strode to one of the small plastic tables, stiff muscles protesting with each step. I rarely wore my shoulder holster. Besides being too warm under jackets—to the point of ruining some of my favorite silk blouses—it rubbed against my ribcage, sometimes making me sore for days. What I was thinking earlier this morning when I put the whole package together? That was just it. I wasn't thinking. I was living moment-to-moment, and it was rubbing me raw in ways I'd never experienced before.

Another uncomfortable spot in my jacket erupted as I waited for my sundae and I snagged a rolled-up magazine out of an inside pocket. I'd jammed it into my jacket on my way out of the house, fully intending to unroll it and stick it into one of the longer zippered compartments of my briefcase as soon as I got into the car ... almost three hours ago.

I placed the magazine on the tabletop and smoothed it out, nearly salivating at the thought of reading its glossy pages. An acne-laden, carrot-topped boy of about fifteen walked up to my table. I offered him my red-and-white number and he stood before me trembling, the tray he held between his scrawny arms shaking. Poor kid. My cop uniform must have scared him.

I stuck the number on his tray and picked up my sundae and soda. The gangly boy backed into his retreat before I removed my hand from his tray, all the while staring at my ribcage. I really should've locked my weapon in the trunk before hitting the road today.

It was legal for me to travel armed, but it certainly wasn't comfortable, and I was sick and tired of being uncomfortable. I shoveled the first of many giant spoonsful of ice cream, chocolate sauce, and salted pecans into my mouth, waiting for the hit of euphoria to sink in.

Even though it was winter, the cold dessert warmed me from the inside out as I browsed through the magazine spreads of the latest fashions. The extra endorphins flooding my brain eased the tension, but I was hyper-aware of the sharp discomfort of the gun digging into my ribs. Looking around the restaurant, I pulled the pistol out of my holster and placed it between two magazine pages. Sweet relief washed over me, and I finished my treat in companionable silence with my fellow patrons.

Could have been they weren't used to seeing women eating ice cream for breakfast.

CHAPTER TWENTY-THREE

Friday, December 18

The last forty-five minutes of my journey to Springfield flew by. I blasted rock music from the 1970s all the way to the Royal Plaza.

The rest of the day fell in line with my early morning start. Gino's smile floated before my eyes like a precious gem. We hadn't really talked since our rather chilly-ending dinner, and I was eager to clear the air between us. His van sat in the first row as I pulled into the hotel's expansive parking lot. Gino was out of the car before I even had mine in park next to his. His broad smile felt like home, and he shook his head and deepened his smile as I drew near enough for a quick hug.

"Hey, G! I thought I'd be riding with you on this crummy job." I pulled back from him, straightening my jacket and repositioning my briefcase strap on my shoulder. A large man wearing a hoodie stood behind Gino, arms crossed. I jabbed my head in his direction. "This guy taking my cruiser back home?"

Gino nodded.

I handed Gino the keys. "You vet him?"

Gino nodded again. "*Por supuesto*. Crummy? This no is crummy job, m'hija. This is a dream job. Traveling behind a beautiful coach—fully armored and fully loaded—with you at my side. Carrying a pig's pig to a destination he does not wish to see. What could be better than this?"

"The bus one of yours, then?"

"M'hija, they are mostly all mine in this state. And in the next two states."

In addition to designing handcuffs, zip ties, and most other criminal restraint items my own station stocked, Gino's design talents bled over into vehicles and security systems. His products were in high demand before they left the drawing board. The armored bus transporting Cal "Nomad" Terry was one of Gino's latest designs, and I couldn't wait to see it rolling down the highway sporting its first dangerous, yet well-contained, criminal.

"Our ride is parked just outside the capitol building. I go to bring it up for us, and you will meet me in front of the steps." Gino's vibrancy eclipsed his free-style grammar.

"C'mon, cut me some slack, G. How about we meet a block up, in front of the coffee shop?"

"Can I not entice you with an organic smoothie instead? As I have so often stated, you and coffee have become overly entwined."

"Coffee would be lovely. How about we meet in front of our little shop in five?" Triumphant for the moment, I turned on my heel and walked off before he could object again. A favorite little boutique was on the way that ought to be just opening up. If I hurried, I could take a quick tour through its wall of purses.

Gino beat me to the coffee shop and stood up when he spied me from his perch on a stool at the counter. Two large paper cups and two paper bags were stuffed into a cardboard carrier, waiting at his elbow. We walked to the new, white panel van parked in front of the shop, pausing at the passenger door.

"Here, m'hija, *favor de tomar* these drinks for me just a minute."

I took the tray from him, careful not to spill a drop from either cup. As I climbed in, the new-car smell imprinted into the vinyl seats made the perfect backdrop for the unique sights and sounds of the customized van.

Gino was singing some lively Cuban tune as he sprinted ahead with the van, dedicating the next five minutes to catching up to the expensive, "Nomad"-toting, Illinois Department of Corrections convoy. He exchanged nods with the driver of yet another one of his vehicles as the first driver slowed down to allow us to slip into position behind the armored bus. He worked the accelerator for a while, jumping us ahead in fits and starts, until he found a pace he liked. He then settled back, turned up the music and drove quietly for the first hundred miles while I dozed.

Loud buzzing and humming noises coming from somewhere deep inside the engine of the van woke me as we drove through the barren land, rarely straying more than six car-lengths behind the behemoth before us. I'd never seen a bigger bus, and it looked to be brand new. Cameras were mounted along the top of the coach, and there were no windows, making its white sides seem unusually thick, even from this distance. Where did Gino get his ideas? It was all I could do to keep up with the maintenance needs of our vehicles; I couldn't imagine designing one.

In direct contrast to Gino's brilliance was the extreme lack of creativity apparent in the letters announcing the owner of the monstrosity. Illinois Department of Corrections was stenciled in large, black letters on both sides of the bus, and the letters IDOC graced the back panel ... just in case you missed the sides, I guess. I broke our comfortable silence to ask him how much money he made on each bus.

"Forget the bus and the money, m'hija. Today we must speak of the unspeakable. I must hear from you about what you have experienced with that terrible man you married against my will."

So that was how this was going down. I sighed. I should just clam up for the rest of the way. "Well, Gino, it's ... complicated. I ..." I turned my head away to study the desolate landscape flashing by outside my window. "I don't have it in me today."

I tried to stem the tide of his need to know, but the dam had already broken.

"M'hija, you got it all. God has crafted a masterpiece. You are fearfully and wonderfully made in every way. And you got the brains, no? Not to mention beauty, as well. Your talent surpasses that of most men—those who are not so talented as me, *verdad*?"

"Yes, well, maybe, but Gino—"

"You know your way around guns, knives, kitchens. You are every man's dream wife. What could that horrible man be thinking? It makes no sense. But still, I am glad you will be free of him. It will be for the best. You will see. Our great and merciful God has something so very much better for you."

My only answer was more tears. So far, our little chat was not going according to plan.

"Is okay, m'hija, you can cry to me. You need to maybe get it out of your system."

"Where do I even begin? It's a sad story. And I hate it, and I'm ashamed of it, and I wish it weren't mine, but it is." I sniffed and scrubbed a tear from the edge of my eye. "He abused me, Gino. Del is an abuser. He hit me. He did things— nasty things. It nearly killed me, but it didn't. I shouldn't have stayed, but I did, and I wish I hadn't. I guess I wasn't brave enough to leave. So now I'm reaching down deep inside to gather all the courage I can find just to get through the day. That's all I can do right now."

"That's all any of us can do. We only have today. You have to keep reaching for your strength within, m'hija. And as you reach, our great and merciful God is reaching for you. You just don't know it yet." He paused and looked over at me. "I am not loving this new you so much. I want my feisty Chief Josie to come back. I want you to learn you are a daughter of the King of Kings."

Del's face floated before me and, for a moment, my heart opened just a crack. Unbidden pictures of God assaulted me, and my heart turned stony. Anger rushed at me from within, and I raised my voice, clenching my teeth as I spoke. "I know I've got it going on. I know you'll never understand this, but I lost it for a moment—lost sight of who I am for a season. A really long and terrible season. I got hooked up with Del and, before I knew what hit me, I lost myself completely."

"Come back, m'hija. It is time. God calls you gently to Him."

Gino's words were like a hummingbird I'd found one day, trapped inside my garage, banging his tiny body against the garage window. The poor little guy wanted to break through into the fresh air, but there was no place for him to escape. I'd like to know Gino's words, to let them in, but there was no place for them to rest. Gino's kind of calm never seemed to find me. Maybe I'd been keeping too many secrets from too many people for too long. Maybe today I'd start to let the secrets out. One little hummingbird secret at a time.

"On our honeymoon, Del was wonderful. He was thoughtful and charming. He reeled me in by being the man every woman's looking for."

"The wounds are deep, m'hija. But the healing will be deeper."

"The first time he hit me, I was stunned. And I never told anyone. I couldn't." I took off my gloves and stared at them resting on my lap. "We were driving home to Illinois from my family's home in Wisconsin. He was at the wheel. After the honeymoon ... maybe three or four weeks later. He seemed to be angry all the time, simmering like an over-cooked stew. I thought it was me."

"So much pain. So many lies he had you believe. And you— you are the sweetest and the toughest, and well, let's face it, you can also be just a little bit frightening, but—"

"I was so confused. It never happened in a straight line. He would hit me or push me or threaten me, and as quick as the episode began, it would end as if it never happened. In the beginning, I would press him about why he acted that way, and he would cry. He'd beg for my forgiveness and promise never to do it again. Then it would stop ... for a while."

"But nothing ever really changed."

"No, nothing changed."

"You should've challenged right up front, m'hija. Did you not, at the very least, think of it?"

"I couldn't. Every time I thought about standing up to him, I just fell back into myself. I froze—couldn't move, couldn't react, couldn't bring myself to leave him like I should've done a thousand different times. I second-guessed my every move."

"It is so hard to believe. When are you unsure of yourself? You are the wisest, strongest lady I know. This is a side of you no one else has perhaps seen—a side that motherless son of a rat did not deserve! This tender Jo is to be cherished, and this ... this *puerco malismo* should have been adoring you, protecting you. Not ..." He shook his head. His dark-brown knuckles grew lighter as he gripped the wheel so hard I wondered if it would snap in two.

"Gino, I'm okay."

"No, listen to me. A man must never hit a woman, no matter how much she annoys him. Never! Your husband is a coward."

Opening his hands wide, Gino drove as if also making supplication on my behalf. Dreary scenery zipped past the windows as he spoke. "You have made me sad this day with your story. Happy to have you tell it to me, but sad to hear it. Sad, as you had maybe forgotten that you had so many friends. You could have come to me or to Nick. We would have helped you. And let us not forget, m'hija, you have a gun."

"Seems like all I've got sometimes is my fear and my doubts and my shaky second-guessing, but yes, I most definitely still have you, Nick, Mitch, Jim, and Donna on my side. And I need you. I need you all."

Gino's cell phone chirped, but he ignored the text and glanced at me. I looked out the window as a gas station flitted by on my right.

"But why, m'hija? Why could you not stand up for yourself? Fight back? Leave?"

"I don't know. I just couldn't. I just kept caving in."

"Okay, this I can accept. But then, why did he decide to go? What happened to make him cheat on such a beautiful wife as you?"

I squirmed in the seat. A large bag of barbeque corn nuts would be welcome right about now. "That's the wrong question at this point, G. The real question is, how much is he going to hurt me on the way out?"

CHAPTER TWENTY-FOUR

Friday, December 18

I fell asleep again for the last few minutes of the ride, rousing when the van slowed to a stop and the temperature shifted dramatically. Gino had opened the door for me. I did a quick cat stretch and squeezed the sleep out of my eyes.

"You are finally awake? Good! I can't hold this door open for you all day." Gino leaned over me to release my seat belt and help me out of the van.

"I must've dozed off for a minute there. Sorry. What are you doing? Where's the bus ... and Nomad?"

"I'm letting you out here at the front, m'hija. Like the perfect gentleman I am. No need for you to join me for another tour of the seedy side of Paradise County to deposit this animal we're hauling."

"No, I'm going with you. Keep driving around to the back."

"Forget it. I got my orders. And anyway, isn't that your right-hand *mujer* coming around the corner with your ride home?"

I followed the nod of his head toward the approaching set of headlights, fully awake now that the chilly early evening air washed over me. Sure enough, Mitch pulled into the parking spot in front of us as Gino remained double-parked in front of the courthouse steps. The IDOC bus had been surrounded by both the heavily armored county van and two county squad cars.

This was like the fourth of July for some of these guys. Not much happened in our little county during the holidays beyond the occasional domestic violence call. The deputies wanted to get up close and personal with a real criminal while they could. There were often "accidents" in transport, and they happened more often than not as guards escorted prisoners from cell to cell. From the sounds of the voices gathering, there would likely be more than one "accident" for Nomad to contend with tonight. He might've earned it, in my book, but with Gino in the background, the other guys would be kept in line. Gino'd long ago proven his mettle as a local, county, and, ultimately, state cop. Respect as deep as his stayed alive among the boys.

"*Vaya*, m'hija! I gotta go see about keeping the integrity of our boys in blue intact."

"All right, all right. Go be the amazing man you are. But first, I get a hug. Thanks for the truth talk, Gino. You mean the world to me."

"*Vaya con Dios*, m'hija."

I nodded and half hugged the rugged man before sliding out of the van. I leaned in to grab my purse and briefcase before shutting the door and waving him away. He jogged back to the driver's side and jumped in. Flashing the lights, he drove off after the bus, a growing parade of squad cars falling in behind.

Mitch and I launched into the standard news and gossip from her day's shift as I drove her home. We pulled into her driveway for the drop-off without wasting a minute. We were both exhausted.

"Thanks for the company, Mitch. See you tomorrow. Say hi to your hubby for me."

I hugged her before giving her a gentle push toward her house. I watched her walk up the stairs and waited for her husband to come to the door. We exchanged happy waves as he ushered her in, and I pulled out of her driveway.

The front of my home was all lit up as I approached, and for a moment, I froze, a terrifying sense of deja vu falling in around me. But this was something entirely different.

The scene was enchanting. My house was framed in thousands of white holiday lights. The porch was lit so brightly, the fresh paint that livened up the wooden decking and the glass of the porch lanterns sparkled. White icicle lights hung from the eaves, a lit Christmas tree was set up in the living room window and decorations of varied shapes and sizes hung scattered along the length of the front porch. I parked, got out of the car and walked to the front steps to get a closer look. Fragrant green boughs curled around the square pilasters of the farmhouse porch and streamed down the railings.

At the top of the stairs, I nearly doubled over laughing. Shapely urns held a festive collection of plastic rifles, shotguns, and pink, plastic machine guns, each decorated with lively bows of every color, some with poinsettia flowers blooming out of the business end. Hilarious. And beautiful. And must've taken someone a great deal of time to pull together. I grabbed one of the longest plastic rifles with its protruding poinsettia, ran my hand down the length of the barrel and burst out laughing again.

"Dude! What's so funny? Never seen a little Christmas display before?" Jim walked up the steps with Donna by his side.

I hugged them both, still laughing.

"Anybody can do a crèche. I figured you needed something a bit more avant garde." Jim's widespread arms gestured to his handiwork.

"Thank you! Donna ..."

"I had absolutely nothing to do with it. This was all Jim's idea."

"You guys ... I ..." Donna and I just stood there, grinning and crying on my front porch. Jim rolled his eyes and shooed us toward the front door.

Donna smiled at me and reached into her pocket. "Oh, here. Take your house key back. I'm staying here with you two tonight. Think of me as a chaperone. For your virtue. You'll thank me later."

As I opened the front door, an unshaven, wet-haired Nick sauntered down the stairs. "Welcome home, Josie. Like the decorations?"

"They're stunning." I stepped into the living room and gasped. A six-foot artificial spruce, completely decorated, stood in the corner between two of the front windows. I had only glimpsed the Christmas tree from outside, but now I could see the detail and care with which it had been set up.

"You like?" Nick grinned from ear-to-ear.

"I like, Nick. Thanks. Maybe Christmas won't be such a bummer after all."

"Say, Jim," Nick said. "Could you tell me what day this is?"

"Sure, Nick, I'd be glad to. Why, it's Friday afternoon. Practically Friday night."

"Friday night? Really? Hmm. Isn't there some sort of suburban ritual involving pizza on Friday nights?"

Jim nearly danced over to the double ovens recessed into the far wall of the kitchen and pulled open the doors simultaneously to reveal two large, thin-crust pizzas.

Jim waved a slice of pizza under my nose, chasing out all vestiges of resolve, and the party began. We spent hours eating snacks and laughing late into the evening. We even put our coats on and shot a few frigid games of makeshift darts in the garage before the party broke up. By the time I collapsed on the sofa in the great room, my face was sore from smiling. The power of their friendship still surrounded me.

Nick had agreed to stay with Jim and Donna in their comfortable guest room at the urging of all three of us. Designer sheets trumped my basement's sleeper sofa, so I was truly all alone in my big, empty house. It might've been my exhaustion, but in the evening solitude, I felt as if I weren't alone, almost as if Gino's God was watching over me.

As I fell into bed upstairs, I held on to the warm feeling as long as I could, and as I drifted off to sleep, I smiled. I was actually looking forward to tomorrow.

CHAPTER TWENTY-FIVE

Saturday, December 19

I awoke to an eerily quiet Saturday morning. Today marked the beginning of the second weekend after the unthinkable had happened. I smiled. Nothing like having a hot special agent living with two dear friends right next door to give a girl peace of mind 24/7. I stretched out like a cat in my bed as I slowly came alive, limb-by-limb. Morning sun flooded my room, the warmth reminding me so clearly of my Magnificent Being's brilliant presence that I half expected to see Him materialize before me. The thought came to me in a flash and then dissolved, but His peaceful presence stayed with me. Maybe I needed more sleep. Maybe I was hallucinating. Maybe if I stayed in bed a little longer, He would come to me in a new vision or dream.

The airplane motor sounds of coffee beans grinding convinced me to get out of bed, toss on my jeans and hoodie, and head downstairs for a little surveillance. I'd programmed the coffeemaker before I went to bed, a small semblance of normal returning to my world. I'd even placed Nick's navy FBI coffee mug next to the machine, along with my requisite two packets of sweetener.

I'm home. Smiling, I opened the fridge. Nick's handwriting on a note he'd taped to the large carton of heavy whipping cream before his departure last night, left me instructions to be careful and check the door locks twice.

I poured myself a cup of coffee, doctored it to perfection, and headed over to the comfy sofa. The saxophone sound of my phone rang softly inside my purse, and I rooted around in the bottom of it. Unfortunately, a cop was always on-duty. My grumbling turned to squeals when Georgi's name appeared on the caller ID. I hit the little green icon.

"Hey, Georgi!"

"Hey, Jo! How are you, girl? How you holding up? Cliff and I are worried sick about you, and we really want to see you. What're you doin' today? You're not working, are you?"

"The day is all mine." I took a sip of coffee and almost purred like a cat.

"Great."

"Why? What's up?"

"You had breakfast yet?"

"Nope."

"Good. You dressed yet?"

"Yup."

"Perfect. You had your first cup of coffee yet?"

"I'm on it. I may even have two or three before I'm through."

"Pour it into a travel mug and get your lazy butt off that sofa. Cliff and I are taking you out to breakfast, so get moving. We're starving, and you can stand a few hours off-duty over the border."

She probably wore her trademark triumphant smile as she hung up the phone without giving me time to reply. Looked like I was headed to Wisconsin.

Fifteen minutes later, I pointed my pickup truck west and north, waiting for the heat to kick in as I shivered in the frigid morning air. I put my portable coffee mug down only long enough to find acceptable tunes on the radio. It was just past seven a.m., and the drive time would easily be cut down by a third because of the early hour and the breezy feel of Saturday morning traffic.

Perfect day to cruise up north to see my people. I would not let family members know about this quick trip—it'd take what little spare energy I had to fill Georgi and Cliff in on this new chapter of my life's story. That part of the visit would not be pleasant but, at the same time, it'd be nice to get it over with.

Rolling past the border, through sparse traffic on I-94 North toward Milwaukee freed my thoughts to wander. Given Cal "Nomad" Terry's capture, and the hunch he was likely the Mentor Sister Serial Killer, all movement on the manhunt had come to a standstill. But were the Mentor Sister Serial Killer and Terry the same person?

I didn't buy it. It was all too lucky and tidy. Was the killer really behind bars? And the unthinkable—if Cal Terry wasn't our killer, did the real killer already have another woman?

Another woman. I snorted. Images of Del floated out next to me, demanding my attention. I pushed them as far to the back of the truck as possible, but they crept right back into the front seat with me. One of the last times I had traveled this stretch of highway, Del had been with me.

CHAPTER TWENTY-SIX

Saturday, December 19

The window was barely open, letting in some of the glacial air to help keep me awake. I approached Madison's city limits shortly after eight-thirty a.m., shaking my head to dislodge the bad memories of Del and our accident. I was on a new road now—safe, away from him, and heading toward my homeland that recalled simple days spent riding horses, skipping school, and cruising the lake with my buds.

The night Georgi and I watched from the bleachers as Cliff made school history with the winning touchdown, clinching the conference title. That was the moment Georgi turned to me and swore she'd marry him one day. And I was by her side at the altar two years later when she did. Nineteen years old and right out of high school. I thought she was crazy, but I still stood beside her, both of us dressed in our finery, holding bouquets carefully crafted by one of her cousins. And now, years later, theirs was the happiest, strongest union around.

An hour later, I slowed down to take the ramp to Highway 33 at a reasonable speed, turning right at the stop sign. Passing through the narrows between Baraboo and Portage, I surveyed the stark beauty of the Baraboo bluffs flanking either side of the two-lane road. I'd spent many fine days horseback riding up and down those steep, rocky hills. They were a key part of the center of my life, my world.

Soon, I would park at the hundred-year-old Victorian frame house on Fourth Street that Georgi and Cliff had called home since their wedding day. They'd bought the house from Cliff's grandmother, one month at a time. I had thought it confining and old and horribly small-townish. Now it seemed like paradise. Were there any new touches and additions they had created together? How had they decorated for the holidays?

Georgi's decorator eye, teamed with Cliff's fine craftsmanship and attention to detail, had transformed the little house into a highly sought-after retreat. Over the years, they'd turned down offers that could fund small countries.

Cliff must have been on the lookout as I parked on the street in front of their lovely home. He opened the front door as I climbed the first step of the front porch. A brass bugle nestled in fresh greenery adorned the front door. Georgi had also hung bugles of different sizes, artfully entwined in long-needled swags, along the porch railing and from the eaves on the low-slung roof. White lights ran the length of the garland decked with large, red bows, along with clusters of red berries between the bugles and bows. As Cliff opened the door wider, Georgi hustled in the background, locking their two large Labrador retrievers in the kitchen and then grabbing two leather coats.

"Hey, Jo! You look amazing!" Georgi's hug melted me. We skipped down the stairs while Cliff locked the front door and trailed behind us toward my extended-cab truck.

"Nice ride. Can I drive?" Cliff zipped his coat and headed into the street toward the driver's side.

I laughed and tossed him the keys. Georgi headed toward the back, shaking her head and carping at her husband. I relaxed in the passenger seat, thoroughly enjoying Cliff's pleasure as he drove the few short blocks to the Good Eats Café. Bracing against the wind as we crossed the parking lot, we grabbed hands as we jumped over the curb and ran under the awning to the café door. We huddled inside the tiny vestibule behind a short line.

"Good grief, guys. I haven't been here for at least a hundred years. I can't believe how much this place has changed. It's so elegant now."

Cliff pulled off his gloves. "New owners. Put all kinds of money into it. Probably losing a ton of dough. Gotta have some pretty deep pockets is all I can figure."

The place was packed. These were the sounds of my hometown. I smiled and looked around the room, studying the patrons. Most of them looked vaguely familiar.

Georgi brushed off the back of Cliff's jacket with one of her mittens. "You don't know that, Cliff. They might be doing just fine. In fact, I've heard they're way past breaking even. There's even talk of expanding. Might buy the store next door since the electric shop is gone. It's been on the market for nearly a year now."

A large man in a chef's apron appeared out of a swinging door on the right and motioned to the hostess, who immediately seated us in the one empty booth, raising the ire of the others waiting in line before us. Cliff and the man in white nodded warmly to each other.

The waitress filled Cliff's cup with hot coffee and placed a small glass of orange juice in front of Georgi. I turned up my own coffee cup and smiled my thanks as she poured.

"Good to see you again, Miss Jo."

I looked into her eyes but I wasn't coming up with a name. Vague images of a slender runner dashed through my mind's eye as she darted off to the counter. "Georgi, who—"

"That's Timke's little sister."

"That's Timke's little sister? Boy, are we getting old. She was what, about five years behind us? I remember you babysitting her and us coming over to clean out the fridge every now and then."

"Yeah. And I got blamed!"

"You've made up for it nicely though, dear." Cliff gave her a sideways hug as he spoke, limiting her ability to slug him in the shoulder.

"Anyway, since when has this place gone all yuppie haven on us? What's with the brass railings and ferns?" I looked around at the nouveau design, shaking my head.

"Hey. That may be true about the ferns and all, but you really have to give 'em credit for restoring the ceilings, floors, and wood trim in this place." Cliff snapped open his napkin, placing silverware on either side of his plate.

"Okay, I'll give you the ceilings. They're good looking, but who does tin ceilings? I came here for a little breakfast and a lot of gossip. You're supposed to take my mind off my woes. One more line about the décor, and I'm going to have to talk about the Mentor Sister Serial Killer just to change the subject."

"Jo, please—" Georgi's voice rose. She never understood how I could look at dead bodies and not faint. She couldn't even watch police shows on TV.

"Sorry." I opened up a creamer and doctored my coffee. There I went again, ruining a perfectly good morning. I needed to downshift into small talk. "Order the country skillet and a bottomless cup of coffee for me, Georgi, would you please? I'm going to go to the girls' room to splash some cold water on my face and then come back and start this conversation over."

I winked, slid out of the booth and headed to the back. Maybe Nick had an update for me. I slid my phone out of my back pocket and sent him a quick text before stepping into the bathroom.

Any news?

I was examining my bangs when my phone buzzed. Less than ninety seconds. Not bad. My neck stiffened at his one-word response.

Yes.

Oh, no, please don't let there be another one. It buzzed again while I was compiling a response.

You're beautiful, and i miss you. Hurry home.

I blew out a belly full of air and shook my head, already texting my response.

Idiot.

I rejoined my friends. "So, did I miss anything?"

Apparently, I had. Their faces reddened, and they lurched into silence as I slid in the booth.

"What? Spit it out." I cupped my hands around my mug and waited.

Cliff must've been the designated talker. "Jo, it ain't right. It just ain't right."

Georgi grasped my hand after the food arrived. "You know I've had your back all your life, and I'm riding with you through this storm, too. I just wish there was something we could do for you. Is there anything you need, anything at all?"

She held my gaze as I shook my head in response.

"Well, is there anything new you want to talk about with either case?" She read the confusion in my eyes and smiled. "The case of the crazed murderer or the case of the crazy, rat infidel soon to be called your ex-husband."

I snorted. "Where do I even start? It's all bad. It's truly all bad. Del's getting all my stuff and his girlfriend, and I'm being taken to the cleaners. End of story." I'd told my woes to so many people in the past few days, I could recite them in my sleep. But it did take away my appetite. Not entirely a bad thing.

"That ain't right." Cliff was indignant.

"No, it ain't. But it ain't changing anytime soon, either. And I don't know what else to tell you. I'm just trying to keep my eyes on the prize. Stay safe, sane, and available to Samantha, and keep putting one foot in front of the other. And then remember to wake up and keep doing it again the next day. But I'll tell you this: I'm blessed in the middle of this storm. Don't get me wrong. I hate everything that's happening. It seems so surreal. But in those moments when it's all going down in front of me, here's what I see—you. Both of you and all my amazing friends. Warm and loving and present and everything I need, just when I need it. And what kind of crazy great news is that?" My heart opened wider as I recounted the truth of the blessings I'd experienced since my world turned upside down.

"Nearly as crazy as having that terribly good-looking Italian FBI guy in your house, waiting on you hand and foot to hear Donna tell it." Georgi held a fork in the air for emphasis. She stabbed it in my direction. "Aha! Your face is redder than Cliff's shirt! What's going on? Details, please." She put the fork down and leaned in. Cliff rolled his eyes and concentrated on his skillet.

"It's not like that. We're just friends. Colleagues really. He's here on a case and helping me out at the same time. No big deal. Not a *thing*. Not a thing at all." My voice had risen, but I couldn't help myself. I was going for natural and ending up with excited half-shouts.

"Methinks the lady doth protest too much." Cliff was back in the game now too. "You could do worse, Jo. Just sayin'. Looks to me like Del's gone for good."

Georgi and I stared at him like a snake on the kitchen floor.

"Cliff!" We shouted his name in unison. We startled ourselves and laughed a good long time. And we kept it up through the skillets, egg-whites and all.

By the time we'd finished breakfast, it was nearly noon. Cliff wanted to head to the Farm and Fleet, while Georgi and I were seriously debating whether to take a quick cruise to Devil's Lake. The lake won, and we dropped him off at home and headed out of town.

Georgi angled herself toward me in the passenger seat. "Are you about ready to come back home? They don't deserve you down there in Illinois. You've already got a great start with your rustic cabin on the lake. By the time you and all of us finish punching it up, it's going to be a beautiful haven. What are you waiting for? Come home."

The roads had only been plowed once this morning, so I slowed to the speed limit as we hit Highway 113.

"I wish. I don't even know what home is anymore—a place of my own that isn't the same without me. Home like you and Cliff have made for all these years in Baraboo. I don't know where that is for me anymore."

The heavier brush signaled our arrival at Devil's Lake State Park, and I drove toward the south shore, easily navigating the winding, asphalt road and sharp turns of Snake Hill. We made our way to the bottom of the country road that runs next to the picturesque lake. Waves crashed against the rocks on this brilliant December afternoon, and we drank in the majesty of the scene. I'd asked Cliff to check on my cabin three days ago, so now Georgi and I could devote our few hours to the beauty of the terrain before us.

Georgi pointed to a grove of trees with the hint of a path submerged between them. "Water's pretty high again this year—been so much rain. You can still see signs of this fall's flooding here and there. The walkway's still covered in water."

"When did they put that in? I like it, but this isn't exactly Atlantic City for crying out loud. What's next? A roller coaster?" I glanced at Georgi and winked as I negotiated around the curves hugging the lake.

"Are you still driving around with your head in the clouds, missing everything in front of you? This thing's been functional for about two and a half years now. You always were looking for what might be up ahead. A new case just waiting around the bend."

"Yeah, maybe." The road led into the campground area. I slowed down as we drove through a deserted checkpoint.

"Maybe that's the gift behind this mess," Georgi mused. "Ever wonder what else you might've missed with all your rushing through life?"

A long sigh was my only answer, and she wisely changed topics before I stopped talking completely.

"So, seriously. What are you gonna do now? Don't be mad at me for saying this, but they're looking for a sheriff here in Sauk County. You could come home to Baraboo. Be like a part-time job for you. You could be our first female sheriff. You'd be a regular rock star, and half your old buddies are on the county board. Got a good feeling you'd be a shoe-in."

"Uh-huh. Wanna walk around the lake? Maybe take a hike, seeing as how it's turning into another one of these freakishly warm winter days?" I steered toward the parking area.

"Thought you'd never ask."

I eased into a spot near the beach, parking in a barely-plowed row with a half-dozen other cars. Most of them sported ski racks on the top. *Wisconsin in the winter.* I shut the truck off and turned to Georgi. "You're not going to pull out a beer or anything, are you?"

"That was your thing, if you remember right."

"Oh, yeah, good point. How 'bout we shut up and hike?"

Georgi jumped out and closed the door. She took off ahead of me, walking toward the start of the path we'd hike. It took me a minute of rummaging around in the backseat to find my sturdiest pair of workout shoes and put them on. I had to move from a jog to a sprint to catch up with her. We walked the length of the parking lot in silence, side-by-side, until it was time to begin our ascent. She had chosen one of the most challenging trails. I needed to get out more.

It took a little while for us to get back in sync. Once we did though, it was just like those perfect afternoons spent together in high school, matching long strides as we admired every hot boy in the park.

CHAPTER TWENTY-SEVEN

Saturday, December 19

Georgi and I scrambled upward, slipping and sliding along the icy and steep path, until we reached the top, just as the wind picked up. The view of the clouds rolling over the lake was breathtaking. We stood together to take it in, turning slowly to catch the beauty in all directions. She snapped a few pictures and handed me her cell phone. I had just stepped into a clearing to find the best possible vantage point when I realized I hadn't checked my work cell lately.

I whipped it out of my pocket. I'd missed seven calls and five texts from three different people. It must've been ringing off the hook in the restaurant, but I couldn't hear it because of the noise. This could not be good. I punched in my voice-mail code and played Nick's message first.

"Josie, call me back. Now." The six that followed were from him, Gino, and Mitch. My stomach tightened into knots. Mitch's message was next. She'd put it to me straight. And she did.

"Chief, there's no good way to say this. We've got trouble. Cal Terry's on the loose. He broke out of jail sometime early this morning. We don't know how he pulled it off, but we need to know where you are. Nick said you could be in danger."

I plopped down on a smooth rock as I listened to the rest of the messages in silence. Georgi slipped over to my side, watching me take in the news, call-by-call. I looked up at her and shook my head, not yet able to speak. Instead, I glanced at the three strong bars showing on the phone's face, and punched in Mitch's number.

"Mitch. What's going on?"

"Where are you right now, Chief?"

"In Baraboo."

"Chief, you need to stay put. ViCAP matched Cal Terry's prints on your Christmas card to the Mentor Sister Serial Killer. You could be in trouble. And we're checking in with Samantha's handlers every hour. We got this, Chief. You need to stay put for a little while longer."

"That's what you think. I'm on my way."

"You really can't do that right now. It's too dangerous. The Feds are bringing in more manpower. Let us bring him in."

"I don't care. I hear you, and I appreciate you taking care of my girl. I get your concerns. But you're talking about my territory now. I'm not backing off. We're tracking him down, and I'm leading the charge. I'll see you at the station in two-and-a-half, three hours, max." I ended the call, stuck the phone back into my pocket, and then looked up at my lifelong friend. I held out her phone for her.

"You want to talk about it?"

I switched into cop mode. "I can't. I've got to go."

"Figured. You want me to call Cliff to come pick me up so you can leave from here?"

"That'd be great." I looked around at the clearing. How much more daylight could I count on?

"On it." She followed my gaze. Was she getting nervous? She dialed Cliff on her phone and told him to pick her up right away.

I looked up at the dark clouds. "We need to go. Now."

"Okay. Let's get moving then. Looks like we have a storm rolling in anyway."

"Georgi?"

"Yeah?"

"Thanks for understanding. It's my job."

She placed her hand on my shoulder, and our glances met for a moment. Her eyes were rimmed with fear, and I was unable to hold her gaze. How long had Terry been on the loose? Had I put us both at risk by coming here?

The pine trees groaned under a strong gust of winter wind, sending a faint whistling sound around the bluff. Goosebumps raced over my body. I grabbed Georgi's arm, and we faced the stony descent together. We'd watched plenty of sunsets from this very spot over the years, but nothing like the dark clouds full of a rare winter rain rolling toward us. As we skidded down the shadowy trail, a heavy threat hung in the air. Despite my cop's backbone, shivers ran up and down my spine and I had to force myself not to scream when a branched snapped and bounced down the path.

We arrived at the parking lot right before a pounding rain could drench us both. Cliff was already waiting for us with a golf umbrella, and bless his thoughtful heart, he handed me a brown paper lunch bag as we hurried to my car. I stole glances over my shoulder, and I caught Georgi doing the same thing.

"Didn't think I'd let you get away without a trip to the Square Tavern did you?"

"This what I think it is?"

"Oh, yeah, baby."

"Cliff, if you were available, I'd marry you myself. Sorry, Georgi."

The three of us embraced in the parking lot for a few moments. The warmth of their friendship and the hearty steak sandwich and potato fries from Cliff got me all the way home in less than two hours.

I might have broken a few speed limits, so the magnetic flashing light I placed on top of my truck came in handy. The municipal plates didn't hurt either.

CHAPTER TWENTY-EIGHT

Saturday, December 19

By the time I pulled into my parking space at the station, tense nerves tremored and every muscle in my body seemed to have gone straight to fight or flight mode. Something else had happened. I could feel it in my bones.

Pushing past the bullpen, I headed straight to the conference room, where the voices of Nick, Mitch, and Gino argued with someone. It sounded like a small army had set up camp in there.

Liz was in. On a Saturday? She didn't speak as I approached her desk. Her eyes were red and her skin splotchy. Not good. We nodded at each other as I strode past and stepped inside the conference room. I shut the door behind me.

I'd expected to see my friends, but I hadn't expected to see men in flak jackets emblazoned with FBI initials. Nick's face was grim. Definitely not good.

Everyone rose, including a man named Stone according to his jacket, who sat on the other side of the table. I dropped into a chair, and everyone else followed suit.

I turned my attention to Stone when he cleared his throat. He offered me his hand. "Special Agent Harold Stone, Chief."

Rising from my seat, I shook his hand. I sat back down. Nick and Stone exchanged furtive glances, and I noted a subtle nod of the older man's head, deferring to Nick.

"Chief." The ominous feeling dug its claws in deeper when Nick addressed me by title. "Our problem's gone from bad to worse since we last spoke. We'll get to the details later, but what you'll want to know first is we have reason to believe this sick freak has escalated and grabbed a little girl this time, not an adult." He paused to let that sink in.

Something horrible had been obvious from the grave looks on everyone's faces and the presence of the SWAT team. My professional-self poured a molten mask over my face, even as my stomach grew rock hard and my muscles tensed to the breaking point. Flight was no longer an option. It was time to fight. An army of warriors grew within me. I nodded at him to go on. Nick looked me steadily in the eyes. There was something even worse he had to tell me. My gaze turned hard, and I gave him a barely perceptible nod.

"Yours," he said. "Josie, it's Samantha. He's got Samantha."

My teeth clamped together so hard I thought they might break. I stared at him, willing away the tears that were coming to both of us.

Samantha. Taken. In danger because of me. I had to find her. My girl. My fault. She was just barely six years old. Spunky and defiant, brilliant and deceptive. I loved that little girl more than life itself. And now, because of me and some sick fantasy Terry was nursing, he had taken her. I gathered my emotions before trusting my voice; it was almost impossible to focus.

"When? How long ago?" My girl. My fault. Stop! I had to stop being a mother and start being a cop. Samantha's life depended on it.

"Three hours. We just learned about it forty minutes ago."

"Tell me." I gritted my teeth.

Stone took over the explanation. He had an annoying voice. "Near as we can tell, he and an accomplice followed her to an early afternoon Christmas pageant rehearsal at her church. The foster parents had dropped her off at the curb, then left. The accomplice grabbed another little girl in front of witnesses and dragged her, screaming, toward a nearby car. Your off-duty pals had him on the ground before he got there."

I moaned, pressing my lips together.

Stone coughed and spoke in low tones. "The officers made a textbook take down and started to secure the scene. By the time they called our field office, they were on their way to the station. We started interrogating the accomplice but he lawyered up."

All the blood drained out of my face. A roaring sound filled my head. "And my girl? Where was my girl during this commotion? How did he get to her? What did he do to her?"

Stone looked me in the eye. "Terry nabbed her before she made it in the door. Must've, because not a witness on the scene can put Samantha inside the church. At all. No one saw her."

Images of Samantha swirled through my mind. She had to be okay. *Please, God, please.* I clenched my teeth and stood up. "How is it that no one saw her? How is it that it took more than two hours to realize she was missing? What about the check-in calls?"

"You can't imagine the chaos. Kids were crying, volunteers were busy trying to grab kids and call parents. It took a while until we knew for sure what we had."

"Giving Terry all the time he needed to walk calmly away with Sam. He's a blender. He'd be quiet about it. He'd have studied her, known just what to say. He probably used—" I blanched. "He probably used my name."

Stone nodded his head. "We didn't even know to look for her for over two hours. Several other kids were unaccounted for during that same stretch of time. One left with his mother, didn't even get inside. Another was home sick. A third was out of state with her family and they'd forgotten to tell the director. Samantha's absence seemed like another random event until we figured out who she was."

"Is."

"Right. Sorry, Chief. We know now the kidnapping wasn't random."

How did this happen? Where are you, Samantha? I know you're out there. Can you hear me? Talk to me! Lead me to you! I promise I'll find you. I'm coming for you, baby. Hang on. I squeezed my eyes shut, and opened them again.

Nick spoke in deep tones I'd never heard before, resonating with pain. "Tell her the rest, Stone."

"So, Samantha was heading to the church pageant rehearsal." His nasal voice made me want to rip my ears off of my head.

"Yes, I know." My clenched teeth snapped apart into a half snarl.

"Right. But so were a lot of other kids. Several other little girls." Stone kept his eyes neutral.

"Pretty bold. Why wasn't he afraid he'd be recognized? Why risk it?" The answers to my questions were obvious even before they fell out of my mouth. Nomad really was the Mentor Sister Serial Killer, and we'd underestimated him all along.

"Good disguise. Nice clothes. Dyed his hair. He totally changed his look. Your men gave us a pretty solid description of two men in the area, thought they were dads. But only one remained for the questioning. This guy's evolved exponentially in timing and expertise." Stone shifted his weight.

"Give me your working profile for him, Nick. I'm up-to-date through the Mad Town incident and the trail he's left during the last year. Tell me about his movements since his escape."

"An insider—a guard—took a bribe. Terry had this all planned before he was ever arrested. We're going to get him, Josie. But we gotta move fast."

The enormity of the situation slowly sank in. *Please let Sam be okay, God.* I could feel her. I could feel her panic. I had to snap into action and pull this team together and find my girl.

Stone cleared his throat to speak. "He studies up on unusual Mentor Sisters. Interesting ones—like you. How he makes his selections is still a mystery, but we've got some strong hunches. He's taken a very keen interest in you, Chief Oliver. And you fit the profile of his vics."

Not a profile I ever thought I'd fit. I needed Stone to finish this string of horrid news. "Go on. Let me hear it again."

"He seems to find attractive, successful, powerful women who have chosen to give back to the community by adopting or taking a little girl under her wing. Some have been actual adoptees, some have been foster children, and some have been connected loosely through a religious organization. Others have been linked through the classic program where adults mentor a disadvantaged child, or something similar such as we have here. Doesn't matter. It's always the same. Hasn't hurt a girl, so far. We haven't yet figured out why he might have gone down that path, but we will. You know these first twelve hours are critical."

Not true. Those lost, precious, first minutes were critical. Nick and I exchanged glances. He was thinking the same thing. My impotence in this moment, when up against such a demonic force, made my hands shake.

"We've got to catch this evil monster. Now." I had to keep the team focused.

Just as Stone opened his mouth again, the phone rang.

I looked at Nick briefly before turning on the speaker phone. "Oliver."

"Hello, Chief. Cal Terry here. How are you today?" Terry's voice was creepy. He had a slight southern accent, and he spoke in hushed tones. Surely I would remember meeting someone with a voice like that.

"I'll be a lot better once I have your scrawny neck in my hands and you feel me crushing the life out of your useless—"

"Why, Josephine! You flatter me with your attention. If it's any consolation, Jo, I can't wait to get my hands on you either." His voice grew harder as he finished his last sentence, causing the muscles in Nick's jaw to tick.

"Listen, you soulless monster. You touch a hair on her head, and—" I was breaking protocol the moment I opened my mouth.

"Oh, I will, Chief. I surely will. And then I hope to do the honors with you as well. Ta-ta for now."

The line went dead before I could find a way to lure him out. I'd lost my temper. I knew better. I'd netted no real information. By any standard, FBI or otherwise, I'd failed ... miserably. I'd failed Samantha.

Stone scowled at me. "Well, that went well."

CHAPTER TWENTY-NINE

Saturday, December 19

Stone took this as his cue to impose a break. Jerk. We had no time for breaks—not until my girl was home safe. My hands itched to be around Stone's throat to squeeze some sense into him. I'd been there less than an hour, and already I'd botched things up. I might've ruined everything. I might've cost us a life—not just any life—Samantha's.

I could not let that happen. I needed some time with my team to brainstorm. Maybe Stone's imposed break was a good idea.

"Let's take fifteen." I glanced at those people I trusted.

Samantha. The soft sound of her little voice whispering, "I love you, Jo," before dropping off to sleep during a camping trip. Her golden laughter the day I showed her where Scooter liked to be scratched. The shining hope in her eyes when I promised her life could be better than what she'd seen so far.

Liz slipped in with fresh coffee and bagels for everyone as soon as the door opened. She winked at me with tired eyes as she drove Stone and the SWAT guys out like a herd of cattle. I mouthed my thanks as she closed the door behind them. I waited until it was just the four of us—Nick, Gino, Mitch, and me.

"Nick, we need a plan—and fast. I am not going to sit here while Samantha is in danger. We've got to get men out to the forest preserves, to the playgrounds, the old fairgrounds, maybe even to the Paradise County Civil War Site."

I was listing what could be construed as likely body drops in our neck of the woods. Each area would offer plenty of room and isolation for Nomad to do his evil work. Where else to start?

"We've covered that ground, Chief." Mitch was already on the job. I had discounted my team far too much. "We've got K-9 officers combing all those places. We're sending teams out to the lakes and dog parks too. I've also doubled the security on your mother."

"I'm sorry. Of course you have. You love Samantha too—all of you. And thank you for thinking of my mother." I looked around at them, and tears surfaced as I locked eyes with Nick. We had to find a way to make the best use of our considerable talent. I was failing them. We were failing her. I didn't know what else to do.

I did know, though, what the Mentor Sister Serial Killer had done to his victims. I didn't want to think about it. I couldn't.

Nick stepped into the void my silence created. "Look, we need to take a deep breath and be grateful for what we do know. Let's start there."

We all turned and stared at him. Gino, in particular, seemed impressed with Nick's suggestion at such a time as this. That was usually Gino's territory.

"For starters, let's remember that he has never killed a little girl." I turned away from Nick, eyes stinging. "No, listen to me. We're forgetting something. He has escalated but he has a pattern, a very distinct pattern. He isn't going to veer off of ritual now. This is too important. This could be the mother of all kills for him." Our confused faces seemed to disappoint him as he soldiered on. "Think about it. He plans his kills. He hasn't varied that part so far, and he's not going to vary now. Everything he's done up until he got clipped was precise."

I sucked in my breath. So that's where Nick was going with this. Sweet hope hung in the air.

Gino looked thoughtful. "So what you are saying, or better put perhaps, not saying, is that in targeting our Josie, while he has taken a wide turn off course, our *querida* Samantha is not the intended victim."

"I agree." Mitch's quick joy turned to anger.

"It's me he's after."

"Yes." All three of them answered in unison.

Liz knocked twice and then opened the door, ushering in Stone and his team. A plan was forming. It would be better to have time alone with Mitch, Nick, and Gino to work it out in my war room, but we'd have to settle for the FBI audience. Fair enough.

While we waited for another call, which might or might not come, every field team reported in, but they had come up empty. We all poured over a map of the area, and then we started over. We couldn't keep walking through sludge like this. Samantha needed us—needed me. We'd learned nothing so far. Exhaustion wrapped itself around me like a shroud. Dark pictures of Samantha in the clutches of a madman gnawed at the fabric of my sanity. If she didn't make it—no. I refused to think about that.

Everything you are is everything you need to find her. Alive. Whoa! Where did that come from?

Peace and power streamed into me, ushering in that same strong presence of God. I breathed Him in like the sweetest fragrance, growing stronger with every breath.

My mind cleared. From the looks and responses of my three amigos, we were all having a similar experience. We were on fire—planning and working together like a crew of highly-trained combat operatives.

"Okay, what do we know about Samantha? Where does she live? What does she love? How does she think? How does she respond?" Nick's simple questions seemed to unlock parts of me that the tension in the room had sealed shut. I answered them as simply and rapidly as he threw them out. Mitch captured all the information on the white board.

"She lives in the northern edge of Paradise County with her foster family. She loves animals, especially cows. And ice cream and chocolate buttercream frosting. Pea soup made in my blender. She's scrappy. And smart. She's quick witted. She's strong. She's a survivor."

"Yes, keep it up," Nick said. "What would she have been wearing at the pageant?"

"A robe. She wanted to be a camel or a cow or a donkey, and she was mad they wouldn't let her. She had to settle for being a wise man. Her stubborn streak made me laugh. I was proud of her for standing up for herself, so I ..." I choked up. Mitch stopped writing on the board. Everyone stared at me.

"So I bought her a little stuffed cow for her to put under her robe during the show—the best of both worlds." The excitement I'd generated died down. But I hadn't gotten to the good part yet. "The stuffed animal's official name was Bert, but she wanted it to be a girl, so she named her Ethel. Ethel is one of those toys with an RFID chip embedded inside. I didn't even know the cow had a chip until I saw Sam had installed an app on my phone that used the radio frequency ID chip to give her access to an online game. I threatened to pull it out. Starter drug if you ask me—gateway stuff."

Mitch popped up from the corner of the table. "Assuming she still has the cow with her, you know what this means, don't you?"

"Can we track the RFID chip? She'd have it with her; she took it everywhere." Assuming she hadn't dropped it during the kidnapping.

I reached for the phone and dialed. Nick was already speaking quietly on his cell phone, and Gino typed on a computer tablet I didn't know he had. Finally, a voice answered on the other end of the line.

"Paradise County Computer Crimes Commission. Bentley, here."

Bentley took fewer than five minutes to call me back after I'd described what we were after. He confirmed the stuffed animals did, indeed, have a radio frequency identification chip. But they weren't the active kind that gave off faint signals every few seconds. They were passive and had to be activated by an incoming radio frequency which had a maximum range of thirty feet. However, the mobile app that integrated with the toy might be able to help us do that. Since that type of toy was currently a huge trend, many parents likely had the app installed on their cell phone so their child could play the online game. That app used the cell phone's antenna to broadcast a signal regularly and kept a record of the GPS location where the phone had received answers from any nearby toy chips. The "Find my toy" function could use all those installed apps to search for any that had had contact with Samantha's cow.

But we would need her toy's ID number.

Could it be that simple? I whipped out my personal cell phone and scrolled through the apps to find the right one. "Okay, I've got the app open. How do I find the ID number of her toy, Bentley?"

"Well, it's probably in the app settings. But if she used your phone to connect her toy, then you just have to activate the Find My Toy feature. Look in the main menu."

The feature was right there, where he said it would be. I ended the call with him and tapped the button, and the screen changed to a whirling icon with the words "Please wait." This had to work. It had to.

Each second was an eternity. But in less than a minute, the app opened a map program and placed a star on the screen. It was just north of Illinois, in unincorporated Kenosha. I gasped. I had driven past there an hour ago. Had I passed his car going in the opposite direction on Highway 94? Was my own phone the one that had received a signal from her toy cow as I drove by?

"I know that spot. It's a private hunting club on steroids. Miles of hunting land and game trails. Not to mention indoor and outdoor state-of-the-art shooting ranges. You'd never know it's there, driving by. Lots of isolated spots, with thick, matted pines growing every which way, would provide the ideal cover, even in the dead of winter. It makes all the sense in the world. There's an ancient hunting cabin edging up to the property line. That has to be it. If Sam is bait to get to me, I would have to know where to find her for his plan to work!"

Does he know my routines? He's been targeting us. A fiery brand stamped those words across my heart. Was that beast holding Samantha captive in a cabin thirty minutes from my own home? Black rage shook through my veins, pounded through my temples, burned through my body. Find. Sam. Now.

We agreed to a hasty plan as Mitch contacted the canine teams and deployed them to Wisconsin. Gino ordered one of his secure transport trucks to meet us at the clubhouse. Stone jabbed numbers into his phone and a second later, he barked orders for a helicopter.

We were going to make it. I could feel it. An electric buzz seemed to emanate from my inner being as we raced out the station doors. The bright moonlight was a shock, as was the unexpected blast of warm, moist air. With the odd weather we'd been having, the thick layers I'd piled on under my Kevlar vest could become a problem. But personal comfort was a luxury I didn't have at the moment. Would we find her in time? We had to. Desperation fueled my need for speed as Mitch and I jumped into my squad car and squealed out behind Gino and Nick in Nick's FBI SUV heading north. *Don't screw with my family. We are going to get my baby back.*

CHAPTER THIRTY

Saturday, December 19

We crouched in the woods near the cabin, my lower abdomen pressed up against the unyielding leather of my gun belt, a small roll of fat leaking out of the bottom of the Kevlar vest encircling my upper body. It might not be a bad idea to up my fifty-crunches-a-day regime now that I was staring down the double barrel of forty. Or maybe just start doing them. The polyester fibers of the uniform I had donned melted into the cover of the Kevlar vest, and I didn't care what the care tag read—polyester did not breathe well. We'd been wearing this gear longer than I wanted, but it fueled my anger and gave me a sense of power.

Nick's nudge snapped me back to full attention. Stone was on my left, and Nick and Gino squatted on my right. Each clasped an AR-15 aloft and in ready position. I held my trusty service pistol in my right hand.

A SWAT team crouched behind us, ready to storm the building. All in all, power was on our side. Firepower, manpower, enough power to take out this evil monster. The breaching team slipped into place, shouldering their battering ram as if it weighed no more than a fringed rug. The lead man gave me a thumbs-up and waited for my signal to charge. Thanks to Nick, the Feds had given up trying to wrestle command away from me for the take down. This was personal. My girl. My call. My case. Mine to win, lose, or die trying.

There were no windows in the heavy wooden door of the cabin. We probably hadn't given ourselves away. The terrible pressure of knowing every second was life or death for my little girl bore down hard on me. And she would be my little girl— she *was* my little girl. Pending divorce or no, the paperwork would start tomorrow. The adoption was a done deal in my heart. I lifted my head, gave the nod to the breaching team, and unleashed hell on the demon inside.

Everything happened at once, like a well-choreographed dance. The moves went down exactly as we'd planned on the drive over. The door gave way after one swing. I was the first one into the room, with Stone, Nick and Gino on my six and dozens of cops and agents waiting outside. The entire operation unfolded in a smooth, free flow of room-clearing tactics. Men peeled off in all directions, securing the small dwelling in seconds. We located the perp in the back of the old cabin, up against the wall, bent over a toolbox of metal tools. A little heap rested on a dirty mat on the floor, at a ninety-degree angle from the killer. Please let her still be alive.

My team and every rifle bore down on Terry. I kept my pistol trained on him in a two-handed stance, glancing up from the tiny figure on the mat on the floor next to Terry.

Nick ordered Terry to put his hands on his head and stand up. When the perp turned around, a strong, terrifying evil swirled around me as his eyes locked onto mine. I might've been okay if he hadn't done the two things at once. He smiled. He smiled and then he lunged for my girl. Samantha screamed and her terror echoed through my heart, spurring me forward. The moment he bent his knee and sloped toward my Samantha lying helpless on the mat before him, I squeezed the trigger. Twice, in rapid succession.

The first shot was low, hitting him in the knee. He crumpled toward the concrete, mercifully falling away from my girl. The second shot caught him in the shoulder. I looked over at Samantha. Safe. Still in the classic two-handed shooter stance,

I stood directly over the killer writhing in agony before me. Then I pulled back my right leg and kicked him in the ribs with my steel-toed boots.

Satisfied, I stepped over to Samantha. Her little chest moved with ragged breaths. Paramedics were ushered in and surrounded her. I stepped away from her to give them enough room. I looked down upon her shuddering frame and thanked the God I did not understand for keeping her alive.

And then I lifted my head.

From somewhere deep inside, I emitted the growl of a she-wolf.

I trained my gun on the evil man on the ground. His eyes were black orbs. He didn't talk, but he smirked. I inched forward, finger hovering over the trigger, wanting nothing more than to pump him full of lead until he stopped smirking, but Nick gripped my shoulder to stop me. Gino flipped the Nomad over on his stomach and secured him in a prototype restraint he was beta testing.

I holstered my pistol and sank to my knees at Samantha's side. The medics opened their circle for me. Samantha's fearful eyes locked on mine, and she whimpered as she reached for me.

I took her shaking hand and looked into her eyes. "It's all right, sweetheart. You're safe now. I'm here." I kissed her head gently and smoothed her hair. "We're all here for you, Sam. He can't hurt you anymore."

She clutched my hand to her chest and started to cry. The paramedics had started an IV, and as a sedative took effect, her body relaxed into me, her grip loosening. I held her hand until the sedation pulled her under, and reluctantly allowed the medics to prep her to leave.

I rose and turned around. The Nomad had been removed to one of Gino's custom criminal transportation trucks. Gino, also gone, might even be the one driving the Nomad to the hospital before heading back to my police station. Stone and

Nick exchanged glances of relief. I'd be in trouble for kicking Nomad when he was already down. Possibly big trouble, given the size of the audience. But it was totally worth it. We had done our jobs and gotten it right.

CHAPTER THIRTY-ONE

Saturday, December 19

While exploring the killer's lair, we made a sad discovery in a duffle bag—trophies from Terry's victims. Compassion and sorrow shot through me at the sight of a locket, an earring, and other treasured items of the women whose lives ended way too soon. I was grateful—the evidence techs would have a field day with the bag and its contents. My heart was with Samantha though. Maybe I should be with her when she woke up.

Nick tapped me on the shoulder. "Let's go."

He took my field notebook, closed it and pointed a gloved finger toward the door. I followed him out and let him lead me to the car. Exhaustion seeped out of every pore. He hugged me with tenderness. My arms folded around him, and the warmth of his body renewed my energy. He kissed me on the forehead and gently tucked me into the seat.

"She's going to be okay, Josie. And so are we." He went to the driver's side of the car and got in. He sat there, taking me in with those intelligent eyes.

He pulled off his gloves, reached out his hands for mine and waited. I pulled mine off and closed my eyes, peeling away the horrors we'd just seen. I opened my eyes, reached out to him, and took his hand in mine. "I know, Nick. I feel it too. And all I can tell you is not yet. I'm married. For now."

I closed my eyes and gave my head a shake.

My jeans were encrusted with mud and filth, my gloves were smudged with who knows what, and I'd touched things and people I'd rather not think about.

Nick had pulled strings again, and Sam had been flown by FBI helicopter to the best hospital trauma unit in northern Illinois. Nick drove us southward at about a thousand miles an hour while Mitch stood guard over Sam and texted us updates. When we finally arrived at the trauma center, we were ushered straight to the emergency room. I grabbed Nick's hand and pulled him near me.

"Nick, I'm scared to death to see her. What if she blames me?" My voice broke. "What if she'd ... what if ..." Shudders worked their way up from my gut, and my shoulder blades trembled.

Nick pulled me into him. "Josie, no, no, no. You saved her life. She knows that. You saved her life. You love her. She loves you, and she needs you. Now, go to her."

He gave me a gentle push in the direction of her room. Nick veered off to the nurse's station to get an update on Sam's condition while I made a beeline to her bedside, giving Mitch a quick hug on my way past her. Sam's small frame was sheathed in blankets, and a bandage covered her right cheek. She slept peacefully. The softly beeping monitors around her indicated her tiny body was stable. I'd tried so hard to give her what she needed most—a loving mother figure—and I'd nearly gotten her killed.

I placed a trembling hand on her head. Her eyes remained closed. Her breathing didn't change. *Please, God. Please take care of my little Samantha. Please heal her.* I didn't know what to say, how to pray. I willed her to get better, to forgive me. What kind of mother could I possibly be to her? I kissed her on the forehead and smoothed back her hair.

Nick grasped my shoulder and came in close enough to whisper while looking down at Sam. "It's all good, Josie. It's all good."

He punctuated the news with a quick shoulder squeeze.

I pulled away with a start. "What did they tell you?"

"She's exhausted, dehydrated, she's badly bruised, and she suffered a sprained wrist. While the SOB did rough her up pretty badly, he didn't ... he didn't ..." Nick turned his face away and gulped in air.

I turned and put my arms around him. "It's all good, Nick. It's all good." I rested my chin on his shoulder as I held him. "My little girl is going to be just fine. And so are we. More than fine."

I stepped away from him and turned to look at Samantha, my little miracle girl, still clutching the cow.

She would triumph over all that had been done to her. She had to. And we'd all be there for her as she faced whatever trauma the demon had inflicted on her spirit. My face relaxed, and I tipped my head up in silent thanks. I leaned down to brush Sam's bangs up and gently kissed her forehead again.

A small man wearing a large PCFS badge pushed the curtain aside. The man's eyes met mine, and we smiled at each other.

"Hey, William."

Samantha's Paradise County Family Services social worker shook my hand in his grizzly-like grip. He had a ferocious demeanor, but his heart beat for his kids. We stood over her bed, side by side. He linked his arm in mine. "You know I'll watch over her, and I'll call you the moment she starts to wake up. She won't even know you're gone."

My eyes moistened. Steel rods bolting my feet to the floor loosened just a fraction. I wanted to be at the station, to make sure my face would be etched in the Nomad's memory while he rotted away until his last day on earth. But how could I leave my baby? My heart sputtered. I gasped for breath.

William put his arm around my shoulders. "I got this, Chief."

I nodded, wiping a tear away. "Take good care of her, William. Mitch will stay here too, to keep me in the loop."

"Go take care of business, Chief." His voice was raspy, and the look in his eyes was fierce.

Samantha would be in good hands in my absence. I left the hospital, walking beside Nick with a much lighter heart and an iron resolve. "Let's get to the station. Pronto."

I zipped up my coat as we left the hospital. The wind had shifted out of the north, and the temperature had dropped.

Nick kept his hands in his pockets. "Babe, at least go home and catch a quick nap. I know you want to be there to tie up loose ends, but you need to take a shower and a half-hour nap."

He ended his mini-lecture with a yawn.

A shower and a nap might just be the ticket to calming my nerves and steeling myself for the work ahead. The dark streets streamed by as he drove.

"Guys like him could be out there by the dozen, Nick. How do you live, knowing that? What keeps you so, so, I don't know, so you?"

He smiled and placed a hand on my shoulder. "You, babe—you." He dropped me off at home, and I caught an hour's nap before showering, changing, and returning to my police station. Nick was already there.

CHAPTER THIRTY-TWO

Sunday, December 20

Later on that morning, I tried to review crime-scene photos, but they were too much. I had to leave the folder behind and run to the bathroom in a hurry. I kept seeing myself, or worse yet, Samantha, in place of Terry's other victims. The brutality was unimaginable—a depth of wickedness I couldn't fathom.

Evil had entered my world, and there'd been nothing I could do to prevent it. I was doing my best to be present in the aftermath, taking back control of my station, my village, my universe, and standing up for my officers in the midst of the horror. It was the hardest work I'd ever done.

"Josie, you're gonna want to be in on this." Nick's eyes narrowed as they met mine when I left the bathroom. I followed the slight nod of his head toward the interview room.

He's in there. The cold metal doorknob awoke the cop in me.

Cal Terry, AKA the Nomad, looked up and tried to rise from his chair, but as soon as he moved, two guards emerged from the shadows and pushed him back into his seat. His hands were cuffed at the wrist, and he was chained to the floor by an ankle cuff. A receding hairline littered with wisps of what may have once been blondish hair rendered him unassuming. Where was the gravitational pull toward him coming from? He was like a vortex of evil.

His head was bandaged, and one cornflower-blue eye was swollen nearly shut. The arm attached to the shoulder I had shot was in a sling. The knee I had shot was wrapped in a mess of compression bandages. I sat down at the table next to Nick.

Terry stared past me as he spoke. "In the South, we rise for women, ma'am. Especially beautiful women."

"So, Nomad, why don't we pick up where we left off?" Nick snapped his notebook open and shut a few times to get the perp's attention, but Terry seemed to have set sail for his own world. Was he on painkillers for the gunshot wounds? Or was he out of his mind in pain? His eyes hadn't left the wall over my shoulder.

I crossed my arms and leaned back in my chair. Why hadn't he asked for a lawyer yet? "What, you think this is a bad first date? Why don't you tell me all about yourself? Let's start with the lady in blue. And don't leave anything out."

"I already told your associates my story, ma'am. And I think you know. You were there. You came to me, after all. I knew you would. He said you would." His voice was high and soft, and he whispered half of what he said as though he wasn't sure if it should be said. "But I'll tell you again, if you like. Fact is, I'll tell you anything you want."

His Adam's apple moved up and down as he spoke. His slight southern accent added a sense of menace to his words.

"Why don't you start at the beginning? With the shower." Nick's voice was impatient.

Terry's face turned bright red, and his arms developed a tremor. A strong odor wafted our way. Was it fear—or death? Nick and I exchanged glances.

I nodded at the perp. "Please. Tell me your story, Mr. Terry."

He jerked his head, tearing his eyes away from the wall and staring straight down at the table in front of him.

"It happened in the shower," he said.

"What happened?"

"He told me. He told me everything."

"Who did?"

"God."

"God?"

"God."

"In the shower?"

"Yes."

His voice was now a whisper, and I fought to keep myself from leaning forward to hear more clearly. "What exactly did God tell you in the shower? Did God tell you to do something? Talk to someone? What did he tell you?"

"He told me all about her." He shifted in his seat, intensifying the odor. Fear. Definitely fear. I stared at him. "The governor's wife." He looked up at me as he spoke, his cruel eyes sparkling. "The woman at the flower table. Wearing the blue wrap."

"What did God tell you about her?"

"That she was bad. And God is good."

"What else did He tell you?"

"That He is good and she was bad, and because He is, she cannot be."

"What do you think He meant by that?"

"That she must die. I must kill her for Him. To cleanse her. She must be cleansed by death so that she could stand in His presence in the afterlife."

He looked me in the eye, and his lips curled into a sneer. Evil burned brightly in his foul eyes. "You don't believe me."

"I might."

"You don't believe me. You don't hear Him."

"Is He here now?"

He snorted and shook his head violently as if to expel a demon or two. "Yes. Of course."

"Is He talking to you now?"

"No. He's listening."

"What is He hearing?" A chill ran through me.

"He is hearing what I will and will not tell you."

"Will you tell me what else He said to you in the shower?"

He paused. His eyes glazed over, and thirty seconds of silence passed before he responded. "Yes."

"All right, Mr. Terry. What did God tell you to do about the bad woman when you were in the shower?"

"You won't like it."

"Try me." Bands of steel tightened around my temples.

"He told me to enjoy her. So I did. I enjoyed her very much."

My stomach tightened. I'd already seen the crime-scene photos and both heard and read his initial confession. When questioned about me, Terry's voice had morphed into a voice-over of an actor playing a heinous killer. I shuddered. He had told of first discovering the family connection between my sister, a prominent home-school advocate and mother of my five amazing nieces, and me. A random event. One day in the life of an average American family.

A picture of me and my six-year-old niece, riding a merry-go-round at a park in Spokane, had been featured in the local papers during a home-school convention my sister was running. Rachel sat in front of me on a beautiful paint horse. The picture had been taken just after she'd started in on an oversized ice cream cone. We were both smiling, hair flying behind us. I had one arm wrapped solidly around my happy little niece, while the other clutched the pole. I was in my dress blues, on break after having given a keynote address at the conference. The caption read: **"LOOK MOM, NO SCHOOL."** One perfect day out of a thousand—and he just happened to pick that day to read that paper. And something had clicked for him—tied me into his previous crimes. He researched me on the internet and started his approach near my family in LA.

Would he have noticed if I hadn't been wearing the badge? Had I done anything at all to attract his attention? I'd never know. I didn't need to hear any more. Who cared why he did the evil things he did? Who cared how he had selected all his victims and what they meant to him? The FBI could study this monster as much as they wanted. I pushed myself away from the metal table and nodded toward the one-way glass as I rose to my feet. This interview was over.

CHAPTER THIRTY-THREE

Monday, December 21

I had an initial divorce court date the following Monday morning. The events of the past several days along with spending time with Samantha had taken up every spare ounce of energy I had. Mercifully, it left me with no time to think about my pending divorce and my newly impoverished state. I'd been acting and thinking like a single mother for a couple of days. How did that happen?

My new-found peace lasted through the court appearance. Of course, the fact that Del had not deigned to appear didn't hurt. I wasn't looking forward to seeing him again. Facing his lawyer proved to be annoying enough, in a very costly way. I listened halfheartedly as two grown men argued like preteens over a bunch of stuff they didn't own.

What had we become? I hung around long enough to be polite after the judge issued a continuance, and then I lit out of there before my attorney could wind back up. Gino and I had a lunch date I didn't want to miss.

I'd been thinking a lot about all the life-altering events of the past several weeks and especially about the encounter in Kira's office. That seemed to be the first time I could remember a conscious awareness of God, and I deeply desired to understand what it all meant. Gino was probably the only person I could bring it to who could help me sort it all out.

We'd planned to meet at a favorite Italian restaurant just over the state line. He was already there when I drove up, late, but earlier than my usual version of late. Maybe I'd get some clemency for coming here straight from divorce court. The big man stood up to hug me. After ordering a plate of bruschetta for starters, I gave him a sterile version of my morning and then got down to what was really on my mind.

"Gino, I think I might be cracking up."

"*Tu,* m'hija? *Tu?* Yes, you are and have always been a little crazy—*es cierto*—but only in the most amusing of ways."

It all came tumbling out. My moments, as I'd come to think of them—the dark presence that had plagued me early on, my first encounter with God, and all the sharp twinges of just seeming to know things before they happened.

Gino took it all in, asking me detailed questions along the way, as if I were the most interesting patient ever and he were trying to diagnose a rare condition.

"And this presence, how often do you sense Him with you?"

"A lot of the time, Gino. Ever since. I don't know—maybe since the night of the crash, when life as I knew it came to a screeching halt. And then, in a very real way, that day on Kira's couch. Something's not right with her, Gino. I felt as if God was actually there to protect me from her. I know that sounds crazy, G—"

"Is He here with you now, m'hija?"

"Very much so. He's all around us. I can feel Him."

At this, Gino bowed his head, closed his eyes, and seemed to go somewhere else. He didn't say anything, and his lips weren't moving, so I didn't think he was praying. I hung in there, waiting for him in silence. Still not my strong suit. I looked at my watch and drummed my finger on the table between us. Gino grasped my finger and lifted it from the table, shushing me. I rolled my eyes and waited.

"I saw that!" His chocolate eyes glistened with love. "You are a very blessed woman. I must now tell you of the love of God and of His wonderful plan for your life. And today I am certain that you will be able to hear me. First, you must tell me more of this doubt with which you are struggling."

"I can't, Gino. You won't like how it sounds. I don't like how it sounds. It's all pretty irreverent. I'm not sure you or God will want to hear it."

"And that is where you are wrong, m'hija. That is the beauty of our God. Before you even form the words you feel you must share, He already knows what you're going to say. And He has forgiven you before you even knew you needed Him to do so. So, speak. Share of your doubts."

"Here's the thing, G. If God is this all-seeing, all-knowing kind of God, then where was He when I needed Him? Where was He with Del? Why didn't He stop Del from ruining my life? Huh? Wanna try to tell me that?" An avalanche of jagged rocks tumbled around my stomach. "And don't even get me started on what kind of a loving God would let that monster kill so many women, destroy so many lives. What kind of love is that?"

He watched me intently and patiently. When it was clear I was done for the moment, he took both of my hands in his.

"M'hija, I will not pretend to understand the depth and breadth of our God and why He does what He chooses, or why He does not do what He does not choose to do. It is a mystery to me as well. There is much pain in this world, and *sí*, He could surely stop it. But He is a God of great love and of great mercy, and He longs for us to choose Him on our own. How could you love a God who was more of a genie to you? Who granted your every wish and fulfilled your every desire? Where is the faith in that? But that is not the God of the universe. That is not the God we serve."

"But—"

"M'hija, let us return now to you. He has been calling you, waiting for you. He has allowed you to suffer through some terrible losses and struggles. And I know He could put a stop to these this instant. But something much greater is happening."

He slowly turned his water tumbler and then pushed it away from his plate.

"I have seen how the Holiest of Holies has been using your pain to soften your heart, to open up your spirit to His presence. You are His precious alabaster vase. And your beauty only grows as He breaks you—as you allow His presence to transform your sorrow into joy and your struggles into victories. In the breaking of His alabaster vase, there is much joy and beauty."

My knit brows and grimace spoke before I did. "I don't understand what you're saying. Why am I a vase? What's precious about being a vase?"

"Ah, let me tell you a story. There was once a great and mighty emperor who lived in a very impressive castle, and he liked to surround himself with only the most beautiful people and things. His prized possession was the most beautiful alabaster vase the world had even seen. One day, a small boy came to seek permission to look upon the beautiful vase. The emperor granted this permission, and the little boy was grateful. But the boy accidentally tripped and fell into the pedestal that held the exquisite vase, causing it to tumble to the ground." Gino's eyes grew soft as he spoke. He picked up the root beer he'd ordered and took a long draught.

"As it fell, the emperor panicked, and he ordered his servants to save it, but they could not. The vase crashed onto the marble floor and was broken into a thousand pieces. The emperor was furious and ordered the boy to be arrested for his clumsiness. But then, the emperor noticed the strangest, most beautiful fragrance he had ever experienced coming from the precious oil that had poured out when the vase was destroyed. This precious oil and its beautiful fragrance permeated the entire castle, transforming it into a far more beautiful palace.

"And so it is with you, m'hija. God has allowed some terrible things to happen in your life, but He has made you far more beautiful because of it."

I had teared up halfway through Gino's story. He gently wiped my tears with a napkin and then tossed two twenties on the table. He rose to his feet, holding his hand out to me. I took it, and we walked out of the restaurant.

"I know a place that is perfect for you at this time. A little chapel in the wilderness, not ten minutes from here. I will drive." It wasn't a question.

He held open the passenger door for me, and I slipped inside his car. We ended up at a little wooden church standing in the middle of a corn field. We stepped over downed corn stalks on our way to the steps and found the door open. I followed Gino in and sat with him in one of the smallish, straight-backed pews. I was in the strong presence of God once again, awash in His majesty and peace.

After long moments of silence, Gino spoke. "M'hija, this much is not so complicated. In the beginning, He was. From the beginning, He created us. He created the world. He created mankind to reflect His own face, to glorify Him, to give testimony to Him as the Creator. You can bring yourself back to the story in the beginning? *El Jardin?*"

"Yeah, sure. I mean, I think. Wait, you mean the Garden of Eden?"

He nodded.

"Are you kidding me? I know the deal. God creates the universe. God gets lonely and creates man. Big mistake. He should have created woman first, and He quickly figures that out. So man gets lonely, longs for a two-footed friend, and God creates woman. Woman hangs with man, hears about how wonderful he is and how happy he's keeping the flora and the fauna, and this makes the woman hungry.

"Man ignores woman, opting instead to keep yammering on about how great he is. Woman pretends to listen, grabs an apple, politely shares it with man, and things go downhill in a jiffy. Turns out God is a lover of both apples and obedience. God confronts man. Man lies and blames woman. Everybody stops talking to each other. Bad things happen, and they've been happening ever since. So? You're not really setting me on fire over here. I don't see your point."

"If you were not so busy creating your own stories, I would be pleased to continue." His accent was getting thicker by the second. He was becoming very emotional. For Gino.

"M'hija, if I could, I would fall in love with you, just as you are, looking so very beautiful, with the *espiritu santo* shining so brightly through you and present all over you. But I cannot, so I will just continue to love you as my daughter."

My heart was so constricted that I couldn't speak. I felt the strongest sense of God's love and belonging as Gino's soft, brown eyes met mine. "But you must hear the best part. Though we have all sinned and fallen short of the glory of God, even so He loves you and calls you to Him."

My eyes clouded over. "But all I do is fail. I failed at my marriage. I failed at protecting Samantha. What could God possibly want with me?"

"M'hija, this is when He wants you most. He sent His Son to die for you that you might be saved from your own failures, from your self-condemnation. 'If we confess our sins, He is faithful and just and will forgive us our sins and purify us from all unrighteousness.' He has more for you."

Blood drained from my face as more past failures came to mind. "But how do I walk with the weight of all I've done? How can God want me?"

"He loves you, m'hija. He forgives you. He cleanses you and makes you as white as the snow. He does not see as we see. His eyes are kind and wide and all-knowing. He sees beyond today. Beyond any one moment in time. He loves you and has so much more for you—so much left for you to do. Here. For Him. And for others." His soft eyes shone with life.

"Like Samantha." I closed my eyes and let the truth come to me. When I opened them, Gino stood before me, praying. I bowed my head and joined him. "I know My sheep and My sheep know me" rang through my mind as my spirit snuggled into the arms of the God of Ages, my Rock, my Love, the Most High God.

His nearness drew me to Him, and I found my home in Him. Love and joy rang through me, flooding me with a deep, irretrievable love for Him. I moved into the aisle and sank to my knees. My arms lifted up to the heavens, and I closed my eyes and sang an old Bible camp song that sprang to mind.

Gino joined me mid-song. His shoulder brushed mine as he knelt beside me.

For the second time in weeks, months, years maybe, I felt a true sense of belonging and a solid purpose in my life. I'd come home as I worshipped at the feet of God. The horrors of the past several days fell away as I prayed as best I could to the God I'd somehow always known, but never met. Until this afternoon.

CHAPTER THIRTY-FOUR

Monday, January 4

My over-zealous footwork netted me a three-day suspension, so I spent all the time the courts and Samantha's foster family would allow me with her. Her resilience was amazing. I would be forever grateful for the confident way she looked into my eyes.

Her hand was always locked in one of mine when we left the house. Most of our time together was spent taking little trips around town, visits to ply Max with carrots, playing her favorite games, and baking cookies and cakes together. I was getting a handle on the parenting thing.

In the aftermath of the Nomad arrest, my case to adopt her wound its way through the courts. I shifted my attention to work and spent my first day back in the office enjoying what looked like a few days of relative peace and quiet.

I had nothing on my schedule, with the exception of a mandatory meeting with the one and only Nick Vitallero. He'd actually scheduled a meeting on my work calendar through Liz—a first. Was there another case he wanted my help with? The clock seemed to slow down and almost stop as I waited for him to show up, so I pulled up annual personnel reviews in an attempt to get it moving again by trying to engage my mind in real work.

Nick's signature knuckle-rap announced his arrival. Saved by the knuckles. I shut the report file down and rose, butterflies in my stomach. I opened my office door. Nick stood there in all his glory, wearing expensive cologne and a boyish grin.

"Aren't you going to invite me in?" His velvety-brown eyes sparkled.

I stepped back, inviting him in with a wave of my hand. He looked good enough to eat. For a moment, I thought of reciting the Lord's Prayer, just to keep my mind focused on things above and not on the beauty and the wonder that was Nick.

He walked over to stand in front of one of the leather club chairs facing my desk. Not at all like him. What was going on? I started to sit behind my desk.

"Ah, Jo, would you mind joining me over here?" His gesture suggested I join him on the other side of my desk. Jo? *Did he just call me Jo?* For one insane instant, I wondered if something else horrible had happened to someone I loved.

I walked numbly to the chair next to his and sat down. He waited until I was settled in before sitting next to me. I looked at him expectantly. "Nick?"

His eyes softened as he looked into my mine. Oceans of strength, and hope, and kindness swam in them. I wanted to dive in and bask in that warmth forever. He closed his eyes for a few seconds and then opened them again and cleared his throat.

"So, Jo, I set up this meeting today for a very special reason. I wanted to have a conversation about us."

Us? He wants to have a conversation about us? And he schedules one? Who does that?

"Go on." I decided to play it cool ... if I could. You know, the "less is more" approach. There were so many ways any conversation about us could go.

"Josie." He took my right hand and held it in both of his, sending jolts of love and peace rocketing through me. "You are the most wonderful woman in the world. I admire everything about you. Your tender heart, your new love for God, your search for justice, your wisdom, the warrior in you. All of it, all of you. I admire all of you. And I want more." His eyes were clear. As they stared into mine, I saw hope and a future.

And then, just as suddenly, a black wave of terror threatened to crush me. A dump truck sat on my chest. My pulse raced, and I wondered if Nick could hear it. I bowed my head.

God, I need you now! Please take my hand and lead me through this moment of fear and into Your glorious light. Here is this wonderful man declaring his love for me, and I need You to keep things straight, to show me Your ways, to let me know the right next step.

I lifted my head and looked at the man beside me. I breathed God into the moment. My heartbeat slowed, and my nerves settled to a dull roar. "Perfect love casts out all fear." I smiled into those soft, brown eyes.

"Nick, I've loved you since forever, and I'll love you 'til the grave. As much as I love you, I have to say I love the God who made you more, and I am learning to seek to obey Him first before all others. And one thing I can tell you, I am a married woman. And until or unless that fact changes, there's nothing more that can be done or said between us."

My valiant attempt at putting God first and Nick a close second had not gone bone deep. My eyes were still speaking to him in love. I drew them away from the shining love I saw staring back at me and looked at our hands clasped together. Something on the inside of his right wrist caught my eye—a smudge of dirt?

"Relax, beautiful. I'm not saying I want to marry you … yet. I'm just saying I want to be the first in line when you're ready to entertain the thought. I'll leave the rest up to the man upstairs." Nick drew my hand to his lips and kissed it softly. His sleeve fell away, revealing an exquisitely shaped cross. I stared at it, frowning.

"Nick? Is that a tat?" I ran my index finger the length of it. When had he gotten inked again? And why?

He nodded, pulling his jacket up enough to show the rest of it. Something was written in tiny black script, but I couldn't make it out. Numbers? An abbreviation maybe? I cocked an eyebrow at him.

"'From now on, let no one cause me trouble, for I bear on my body the marks of Jesus'" Galatians 6:17. Let's just say Gino and I spent a little time on our knees at a chapel in a field recently."

My heart raced again. Waves of joy cascaded over me. I wanted to skip around the room like a little kid. I bowed my head and thanked the God of the universe. Then, in my mind's eye, I saw myself alone in a meadow. The sun went down around me, and the heavens opened up, and a beam of otherworldly light shone all around me, connecting me to God in all His glory. He was a shining light of power and love and every virtue packed into one Magnificent Being. I was a minor expression of Him, shining with a powerful light of my own, connected to Him with my heart and soul.

God reached down from heaven and took my hand in His. I looked up at Him in love and trust and awe. Next to Him stood another being of light and beauty and power and strength, also connected from the heart to His light and love.

The power and majesty of God shifted again, and the other being took shape as a man, lit brightly from within, standing beside Him. I couldn't see his features, but I knew the other being was my Nick. Then the beautiful beings turned to face the future and walk together.

The vision faded and I opened my eyes. I tugged my hand free of Nick's and spread my fingers out wide. My wedding band and engagement ring were still solidly in place. Nick took my hand, drew it to his mouth and brushed his lips lightly against each finger. He paused on my ring finger. Then he bent it carefully, making the ring as prominent as possible. He studied the rings, and then he traced the faint trace of a bruise on the inside of my wrist with his finger. His finger trailed back up to my hand, and then he carefully bent the rest of my fingers until he'd formed my hand into a fist.

"I love you, Josie. All of you. Josie the warrior, Josie the lover of small children, and now, Josie the woman of God. I don't know what it all means, or where it will lead us. I don't need to know that today. Having you, having your friendship, is enough for today. And tomorrow. After that, only God knows. And that's enough for me." He gently released my hand.

The glorious warmth of him radiated through me. I placed my hand lightly on the side of his face and nodded. Hope, sweet hope, glittered in his eyes like a beacon in the night.

ABOUT THE AUTHOR

Catherine Finger loves to dream, write, and tell stories. Recently retired from a wonderful career in public education, she celebrates the ability to choose how to spend her time in a new way during the second half of life. So far, she chooses to write books, ride horses, serve others, and generally find her way into and out of trouble both on the road and at home. She lives in the Midwest with a warm and wonderful combination of family and friends.

Anchored by Death (Elk Lake Publishing, Inc) the third novel in her Jo Oliver Thriller series, received the Bronze Medal for the 2018 Independent Publisher Book Awards. Her second Jo Oliver Thriller, *Shattered by Death* (Elk Lake Publishing, Inc) was named 2016 Book of the Year by Deep River Books and was a finalist in both the International Book Awards and the National Indie Excellence Awards. Catherine and her novels have been featured on radio stations, blogs, and in numerous articles—all posted at www. CatherineFinger.com.

Catherine loves to interact with her readers at www. CatherineFinger.com Follow her on Facebook at Catherine Finger, Author, and on Twitter at CatherineFinger@BeJoOliver.

Like to Know A Little More?

About faith:
Would you like to know God personally?
http://www.4laws.com/laws/englishkgp/default.htm

New Hope Christian Community - People, neighborhoods, communities and the world becoming who God designed them to be.
http://www.newhoperoundlake.com

About domestic abuse:
A Safe Place - Transforming Lives After Domestic Abuse
http://www.asafeplaceforhelp.org

The National Domestic Violence Hotline
http://www.thehotline.org/
800–799–7233

About suicide prevention:
National Suicide Prevention Lifeline
http://www.suicidepreventionlifeline.org

THANK YOU!

Thank you for joining me for the journey of the *Jo Oliver Thrillers*! I hope you enjoy reading them as much as I enjoy writing them. Your feedback is always welcome. Please consider sharing your honest review on this and your other recent reads on Amazon or Goodreads.

I love to interact with readers and writers and welcome you to drop me a line at www.CatherineFinger.com

Gratefully,

Catherine Finger

45016233R00115

Made in the USA
Middletown, DE
12 May 2019